# THE DOVES
# IN THE DINING ROOM

# ALSO BY LAURA LAAKSO

*Fallible Justice*

*Echo Murder*

*Roots of Corruption*

# THE DOVES
# IN THE DINING ROOM

## Laura Laakso

2021
Louise Walters Books

The Doves in the Dining Room
by Laura Laakso

Produced and published in 2021
by Louise Walters Books

ISBN 9781916112360
eISBN 9781916112377

Typeset in PTSerif 11pt by Blot Publishing

louisewaltersbooks.co.uk

info@louisewaltersbooks.co.uk

Louise Walters Books
PO Box 755
Banbury
OX16 6PJ

*In loving memory of Elon Pierson,*
*whose kindness, generosity, and sparkling sense*
*of humour made the world a better place.*

# CHAPTER 1

'Yannia!'

At the top of the stone steps, standing next to wooden double doors, is my friend, wearing a flowing sky-blue dress. She waves, and the sun reflects off the diamonds around her wrist. Despite the chill of a clear November day, she is wearing no coat.

'I'm so glad you could make it. You're my lucky charm.'

I smile, a little uncomfortable with the idea of being anyone's lucky charm. 'Thanks for the invitation, Jessika.'

'How could I not invite you, when you're the reason I found my Robbert?'

She draws me into a hug when I reach the top of the steps, and a cloud of floral perfume envelops me. I breathe through my mouth, and the desire to sneeze dissipates. Beneath the perfume, the subtle scents of dust, noonday heat and sun-baked salt identify her as a South Mage.

'Have you heard from your ex-husband?' I ask.

Jessika's hand creeps up to touch a silver line along her temple that's almost obscured by her hair. 'Not a peep since the divorce was finalised. The threat of those photos you took going public is enough to ensure he'll stay well away from me.'

We met almost a year ago. Jessika was one of my first clients. She took a chance on me because there are only a few female private investigators in Old London and she didn't trust her case to a man. I proved not just that her husband was having an affair, but that he was abusing Jessika. After she filed for divorce, we stayed in sporadic contact, though I was surprised by the wedding invitation.

'Good. You're free to move on.'

'Which is why it's so wonderful you're here to witness it all.' Jessika loops her arm around mine. 'Come. I'll show you to your room and then I want to introduce you to Robbert.'

The inside of the country hotel matches the imposing façade. Our steps are muffled by a thick carpet as we make our way up a curving marble staircase. Large oil paintings decorate the entrance hall, and from somewhere within the building, I catch snatches of muffled conversations and soft jazz. The smell of roasted salmon and steamed vegetables reminds me that it has been some time since breakfast.

My room matches the opulence of the building. A large four-poster bed takes up most of the space; heavy burgundy curtains are tied back with gilded, tasselled cords. Huge windows offer a view of gardens and koi ponds. Through an open doorway, I see that the bathroom is appointed in marble and chrome. My eyes are drawn to the fireplace and the stack of logs next to it.

I set my backpack on the floor next to the bed, acutely aware of my scuffed boots and faded jeans. My clothes are clean, but far too informal for this setting. When I turn to Jessika, I smile to hide my insecurities.

'You must be excited about Sunday's ceremony.'

'It's simply wonderful! I can't believe how many people have travelled to spend the weekend with us. The support I've received is more than I ever dared to imagine.'

Jessika turns away, plucking a tissue from a box on the cherry writing desk and dabbing her cheeks. I step closer and rest my hand on her arm, just below a series of round scars that are beginning to fade.

'I'm sorry, I'm being silly,' she says. 'This has been going on for the past few days. Every small detail seems to set me off.'

'There's no need to apologise. It's understandable that you're emotional.'

'Thanks.' Jessika dries her eyes and drops the tissue in a waste paper basket. 'Shall we go and meet Robbert?'

'Let's.' I glance down at my jeans again. 'Should I change?'

'Nonsense. The invitation said to come as you are. What you're wearing is fine, and no one here is going to say anything to the contrary.'

We leave the room, and Jessika hands me the key card, which I tuck into the back pocket of my jeans, next to my phone.

As we are walking down the stairs, a voice calls out to us from the ground floor.

'Jessika, dear, there you are. I've been looking all over for you.'

An older woman in a cream jacket and skirt looks up at us. The curve of her nose and the dimple in her chin resemble Jessika's features, but the press of the woman's lips is severe. She glances at me, and in a tiny flick of her eyebrow, deems me unworthy of her time. My temper flares, but I keep the emotion hidden, although I do curl my hands into loose fists to hide the silvery Fey scars covering my palms. They have almost healed thanks to Lady Bergamon's attention, but I am self-conscious of the marks that remain.

Although she smiles, Jessika lets out a tiny sigh. 'I was showing Yannia to her room, Mother.'

'The hotel staff could have done that. You mustn't neglect your guests. Lord and Lady Warrengton have just arrived and they are dying to get to know you better. These are the people you should focus your energies on, my dear.'

Jessika loops her hand through my arm again as we reach the bottom of the stairs. Her grip causes blooms of pain on my upper arm.

'I'll speak to them as soon as I have introduced Yannia to Robbert.'

Jessika's mother begins to object and then checks herself. 'I suppose you will do as you see fit, though our noble guests deserve more consideration than you are prepared to extend them.'

'Thank you for your advice, Mother.'

The woman reaches to touch Jessika's arm next to one of the marks she bears. 'Wouldn't you be more comfortable with a scarf or a wrap over your dress, dear? I'd hate to see you catch a chill two days before your wedding.'

'I'm not ashamed of having survived Dharren's abuse.' Jessika lifts her chin. 'Are you?'

'Of course not.' She spots an elderly couple entering the reception area and turns towards them. 'Excuse me.'

Jessika waits until her mother is out of earshot.

'Mother was devastated when I announced that I would divorce Dharren. The only thing that thawed the ice between us was my becoming engaged to someone from an older and richer Mage family. Not that it was a consideration for me, of course. I would love Robbert just as much if he was a penniless Shaman.'

I stiffen at the inference, but have learned not to bring it up. For the old Mage bloodlines, the certainty of their superiority over the other magical races runs too deep for me to disabuse Jessika of the notion. She does not notice my silence as she leads me through a set of double doors into a room with floor to ceiling windows. The view of the gardens is beautiful, but none of the people gathered around the room appear to pay it much attention. Dressed in designer clothes and with champagne glasses in hand, they chat, laugh, and make their rounds. I glance back, wondering if it's too late to make a run for it, or at least to go change. What stops me is the conviction that none of the clothes I own would allow me to blend in.

At the far end of the room, a group shifts to reveal a man in a wheelchair. While he smiles and nods along with the conversation, his eyes keep straying to the view, then to the rest of the room. A large golden retriever wearing an assistance dog harness sits next to him. The group surrounding the man moves on, and he spots our approach. His face lights up.

'Yannia, this is Robbert,' Jessika says as we reach him. 'Robbert, I'd like you to meet Yannia Wilde.'

Now that I'm closer, I find him to be older than Jessika, perhaps by as much as two decades. His dark hair and closely cropped beard are both streaked with grey, but it gives him an air of nobility. He is wearing a charcoal grey suit and an azure waistcoat with a perfect cut.

'It's a pleasure to finally meet you,' he says in a quiet voice that holds an undercurrent of strength. When he shakes my hand, his grip is warm and strong. 'Jessika has told me so much about you, I feel as though we are already acquainted.'

The aura around him presses against mine, though I sense no active spells. It takes a mere whisper of power to ascertain that he, too, is a South Mage and a stronger one than his future wife.

'Likewise,' I say, though in truth I know next to nothing about Jessika's fiancé.

Robbert's hand dips into his coat pocket and out again. The assistance dog by his side cranes its head up, and Robbert feeds it a treat.

'I don't know if Jessika has mentioned that I'm a huge fan of detective stories and the heroes of the genre, such as Sherlock Holmes and Hercule Poirot. Perhaps you would humour me by sitting with me at lunch and telling me about some of your cases?'

My thoughts flash to Jonathain Marsh and Tim Wedgebury, but I cover my hesitation with a nod. 'Of course. Though I should warn you, reality rarely emulates fiction. A lot of what I do is boring paperwork, much to the chagrin of my apprentice.'

'Even if that's the case, it will be interesting to hear what your profession is really like.' Robbert leans forward, lowering his voice. 'Besides, it's better than making small talk with cronies who are desperately trying to avoid the subject of my wheelchair. You'd think after all these years, they would have grown used to it, but it remains the metallic elephant in every room I wheel myself into.'

Right on cue, a sharp pain flares in my hip. Rubbing

the spot, I offer Robbert a small smile. 'Sometimes invisible illnesses are less complicated.'

He leans back in his chair, surprise written across his face. 'I didn't realise.'

'It's not something I include in my PI ads. Being one of the Wild Folk makes me enough of a curiosity in Old London.'

'I understand.'

A flash of white in the garden draws my attention to the large windows. At the far end is a wooden structure covered in chicken wire. Within it, white doves flutter from perch to perch. Robbert's assistance dog whines, and he strokes its head.

Behind me, a bell chimes, and I turn to see a butler in a black morning suit holding a silver bell.

'Lunch will be served in five minutes,' he announces.

'Shall we?' Robbert takes Jessika's hand and kisses it.

He leads the way, wheeling himself through the open doors with practised accuracy. Jessica walks next to him, hand on his shoulder, and I follow behind them. We go past the reception desk in the entrance hall and enter a large room with wood-panelled walls and burgundy Persian rugs. My attention is drawn to the large fireplace, stacked with fresh logs but unlit.

Jessika screams.

# CHAPTER 2

I leap forward, eyes roving the room for anything out of the ordinary, when I spot a splash of blood on the pristine tablecloth. As I draw nearer to the long banquet table, a detached part of my mind is cataloguing everything I see. Amidst the crystal wine glasses and silver tableware, two white doves have been arranged side by side. Their wings are stretched out, and a long gash runs from the base of the throat across the stomach. Grain from the gullet pouch and intestines spill out of the wound. Bloodied feathers are scattered around the bodies. Some have landed on the nearby plates and glasses.

From the many footsteps and gasps behind me, the rest of the guests have followed Jessika's screams. Without allowing my focus to drift away from the gruesome scene, I catch snippets of conversations expressing outrage, puzzlement, and speculation that this is someone's idea of a practical joke.

The noise has brought the butler back, and his face pales when he sees the dead birds on the table. He calls for aid, and rushes to Robbert and the sobbing Jessika.

'I can't even begin to express how deeply sorry I am about this. Could I ask you to wait in the conservatory while someone comes to clear the table and take care of the mess?'

Dabbing her streaming eyes with Robbert's silk handkerchief, Jessika shakes her head. 'Who would do such a thing?'

'Whoever it is, I am certain they will be swiftly found out and reprimanded.'

'It's two days before our wedding.' Jessika turns to Robbert. 'Do you think this is someone's sick way of trying to scare us? Do you think someone is trying to stop the wedding? Do you think it's Dharren's revenge for the divorce?'

'I'm sure it's nothing of the sort.' Robbert looks past Jessika at me. 'Though I don't suppose it would hurt to make sure.'

'What do you mean?' Jessika asks, sniffling.

'We have one of Old London's finest PIs standing not ten feet away. Perhaps Yannia could assist the hotel staff in the investigation? She's already familiar with Dharren and the circumstances of your first marriage.'

Jessika turns to me. 'Would you?'

'Of course. It's the least I can do.'

'We'll pay you double your usual rates,' Robbert says.

'Absolutely not,' I reply. 'Consider this a wedding present, though you said you didn't want anything.'

When Jessika tries to argue, Robbert silences her by extending his hand to me. I shake it.

'Thank you,' he says.

'I'll text my apprentice to let him know I'm on a case. If we need any research or legwork done in Old London, he'll be ready.'

'That's right, you've now got an assistant. Should we

arrange for him to come here?' Jessika's eyes flicker to Robbert and back to me. 'Unless you'd prefer help closer at hand?'

'Do you have someone in mind?' I ask, though I am beginning to see where this is going.

'Robbert has read so many detective stories he is practically an expert at solving crimes. Perhaps he could help?'

'I'm sure real life is quite different from the pages of a book,' Robbert says, though he leans forward in his chair, a spark of eagerness in his eyes. 'Besides, having an assistant in a wheelchair will only hinder Yannia.'

'Not at all. I would value your help.'

Jessika glances at the table, the handkerchief pressed against her nose, and her eyes water again. 'I feel sick.'

'Why don't you take our guests back to the conservatory, my dear? Yannia and I will begin our work straight away.'

With the help of the butler and two waitresses, Jessika ushers the guests back to the airy conservatory and organises fresh trays of champagne. Once the doors are closed, the butler comes to me.

'May I ask the staff to clear the table and to dispose of the carcasses?'

'Not just yet,' I say. 'I'd like to take a closer look at the birds first. But while you wait, could you find out who was in the room last and how long ago that was?'

'Of course, madam.' He executes a half-bow, and leaves.

As Robbert wheels himself closer to the table, a grey speck on the rug near to where Jessika was standing a few moments ago catches my eye. I bend to pick up a downy feather. Twirling it between my fingers, I wonder at its meaning. Nothing leaps to mind, and I tuck it in my pocket.

'What should we do first?' Robbert asks.

I join him by the table. 'Let's take a look at these birds.' Hesitating, I glance at his suit and his manicured nails. 'Though if you'd rather not get blood on your hands, you could take notes.'

'Nonsense. Before the accident, I used to hunt frequently. I'm no stranger to handling dead animals and know a thing or two about skinning and butchering fowl. If you move a couple of the chairs aside so I can come closer to the table, I'm ready to get stuck in.'

While I move the chairs, Robbert asks his assistance dog, whom he calls Calleigh, to settle down near the fireplace. Calleigh flops onto her side with a sigh. Together Robbert and I move aside plates and crystal wine glasses for a better view and access to the dead doves. He wheels his chair as close as he can, and takes a photo.

'In case we need it later,' he says.

I lean over the table to look at the birds. Something about the way they have been positioned bothers me, but it's not until I pick one of them up that I realise what it is. The head lolls to the side, more so than I'd expect. I spread out a cloth napkin on the table in front of Robbert and lay the bird on top of it.

'Do you see anything strange?' I ask.

Robbert feels along the dove's neck, a smear of blood transferring to the side of his thumb. 'The neck is broken.'

'Yes. Why bother wringing their necks if you're going to cut them open and spread entrails everywhere?'

'It's more humane?'

11

'That's what I thought. Which in itself is interesting.'

'How so?'

'It suggests that cruelty towards the birds wasn't the point. They were positioned like that to shock us, but the aim was to do so as humanely as possible.'

'Do you think it's a message?'

'Yes, though it's too early to tell who the intended target is and what the message is supposed to be.'

'Are you saying we weren't the intended target?' Robbert asks.

'Not necessarily. It's possible Dharren has somehow orchestrated this or that someone else objects to the wedding. But it could just as well be a disgruntled employee or a customer seeking to tarnish the hotel's reputation in front of an aristocratic guest list.'

'I hadn't thought of that.' Robbert casts a worried glance in my direction, and I am reminded of Karrion. 'It seems I need to think more sneakily if I'm to keep up with you.'

The corner of my mouth lifts. 'I've had plenty of practice.'

Drawing the second bird closer, I examine the wounds.

'See here,' I say, pointing to the neck, where pale yellow skin is visible beneath the blood-stained white feathers. 'It looks like the first cut was across the throat.'

'There was another small cut down,' Robbert points to the throat of his dove, where the skin shows a ninety degree angle of the cut. 'The rest was pulled apart, rather than cut. You can see the unevenness of the tear. That exposed the breast bone, and it was easy to cut through the membranes to expose the internal organs.'

When I lean closer, the smell of the flesh as well as the intestines grows stronger. I am also no stranger to skinning birds. The Shamans who farm the lands that act as a buffer between the conclave and the outside call upon the Wild Folk to help with traditional pest control at certain times of the year. As teenagers, Dearon and I spent many a happy day practicing our archery skills on the enormous flocks of pigeons that gathered in the fields and sending the pointers and spaniels to retrieve the birds we had shot. Although I would never dare admit it to Karrion, game birds were my favourite for many years. Since a Bird Shaman became my best friend, I have changed my eating habits.

'Whoever put these doves on display had some experience of butchering birds,' I say.

Robbert nods, and we continue our examination of the carcasses in silence. After a while, he draws my attention to one of the wings of his bird.

'It's broken. It looks recent.'

'That would have made it easy to catch,' I say.

'But also useless to the hotel.' At my puzzled glance, he explains, 'The main purpose of the doves is to be released from a basket during a wedding ceremony. A flightless dove may be useful for a photo opportunity or two, but probably not enough to justify the upkeep costs.'

Someone else might be horrified by the pragmatic approach to life, but I grew up in a conclave where everything must serve a purpose. Before I left for Old London, I often questioned what purpose I could serve, given that without proper pain medication, I am all but crippled by my connective tissue disorder.

Turning the other dove's head towards Robbert, I

point to the yellow crusty discharge around its eyes and beak. 'I think this bird was sick.'

'Do you think it's a clue? The culprit killed two doves that were probably going to be put down anyway.'

'Possibly. It's something to bear in mind.'

Blood has stained both of our hands, and I dip two cloth napkins into a nearby pitcher of ice water. Robbert takes one of the napkins with a nod and scrubs his hands. I do the same, while taking a look around. There are two doors: one leads to the entrance hall and the other presumably to the kitchen. While Robbert reassures his dog, who has begun to whine, I examine the doors.

'Both of these have locks.'

'Which means that so long as the room was empty when whoever was responsible for this entered, it would have been easy enough to ensure he wouldn't be disturbed while he modified the table decorations.'

'He?' I raise an eyebrow.

'Just for the ease of expression. I make no inference about the culprit's gender.'

'Let's go speak to the butler.'

We find him right outside the door in the entrance hall. The murmur of many conversations indicates he is not alone. I beckon him. Casting a look behind him, the butler slips through the narrow opening and closes the door.

'May we clear the table? Lunch is waiting to be served and our guests are growing restless.'

'I think we're done here,' I say with a glance at Robbert. He nods. 'Did you find out who was here last?'

'Yes. When I came to check the table had been set and everything was ready for our guests, the sommelier was here making sure the correct wines had been laid out. That would have been approximately fifteen minutes before I announced lunch. According to the kitchen staff, no one else came in after the sommelier and I left.'

'Could someone have snuck in from the kitchens unnoticed?' Robbert asks.

'Certainly. Things are hectic during service.'

'How about from the entrance hall?' I ask.

'Again, I expect so. The staff at the reception desk do not recall seeing anyone, but they have been welcoming guests all morning and it is possible they missed something.'

I nod, glancing around the room again. 'Do you have CCTV?'

'Naturally. However, I'm afraid none of the cameras in the entrance hall point towards the dining room doors. The coverage is mostly restricted to the reception desk, the bar, and the grounds in the immediate vicinity of the buildings.'

That is more or less what I expected, and it does not help us. I turn to Robbert.

'Did you notice any of the guests acting suspiciously during the drinks or did you see anyone leave the conservatory?'

'No, but I was busy talking for most of the time. Besides, I have a height disadvantage when it comes to keeping an eye on a roomful of people. However, I cannot imagine any of the guests butchering doves and running the risk of blood stains on their clothes.'

I consider this, my head cocked. 'A black dress or a dark suit would hide it better, but I take your point. It would be easier for the kitchen staff to explain away fresh stains and to clean up. If whoever did this left through the doors to the entrance hall, they would have needed to hide bloodied hands, not to mention a knife.'

'The kitchen door sounds more plausible for both going in and slipping out,' Robbert says. 'Even the most distracted receptionist would surely notice someone carrying two live doves and a knife.'

'I doubt the birds were alive when they were taken to the dining room. It would have been far easier to wring their necks outside and hide them in a bag or a box.'

'Yes, I believe you are right,' Robbert says.

'Can you think of anyone who would want to sabotage an event here?' I ask the butler. 'Any disgruntled employees or guests? Or anyone who would benefit financially from bad publicity?'

'Our customer service is a point of pride to everyone who works here. Any complaints are swiftly resolved. Likewise we treat our staff well. The remuneration reflects the level of service we expect everyone working here to provide. I cannot imagine anyone, customer or employee, who would seek to discredit this hotel.'

'Thank you. I believe we have learned everything we can from this room. Go ahead and remove the doves. Though I would appreciate it if you could speak to the kitchen and waiting staff and ask if any of them saw anything or anyone suspicious during the window of opportunity.'

'I'll let you know.' The butler nods and heads for the door leading to the kitchen.

'What now?' Robbert asks.

'I'm not sure. We don't have a lot to go on.'

'So you don't have a Wild Folk ability that would let you sniff out the person with blood on their hands?'

I bite back a snort. 'I'm not a bloodhound. Even if I did invoke my enhanced sense of smell, the carcasses on the table would mask any residual scent of blood elsewhere in the room. At this point, it looks like the way to solve this case is with old-fashioned detective work rather than with the use of magic.'

'All right. How do we do that?'

'We wait for more information. Though I must warn you, if the dead birds turn out to be an isolated incident, we may never figure out who was behind it.'

'Are you saying that our only chance is to wait and see if this happens again?' Robbert sounds both incredulous and disappointed.

'Up to a point. If something else happens in connection with the wedding party, we can safely assume someone is trying to sabotage your wedding. If, on the other hand, another incident occurs elsewhere in the hotel, it shows that whatever is going on has nothing to do with the wedding and everything to do with the hotel itself.'

'I see.' Robbert nods. 'Yes, that seems logical.'

'You should return to your guests,' I say. 'Jessika will no doubt appreciate your support in fielding questions about what happened. Don't say anything, but be on the lookout for anyone acting out of character.'

'I'll keep an eye out for suspicious behaviour.'

'Not just suspicious. Anyone who seems too calm or even amused by what's happened. Anything that doesn't tie in with what you know about them.'

'Fine.'

Robbert calls Calleigh to him and wheels out of the dining room. I follow him to the reception hall, where a woman in a pale green silk dress is pacing in front of the marble staircase. Upon hearing the door open, she whirls around and hurries towards us. She resembles Robbert; a sister, perhaps, or a cousin. Either way, she doesn't spare me a glance.

'There you are, Robbert.' She crouches by the wheelchair, a hand on Robbert's shoulder. 'Are you well? How do you feel?'

'I'm fine, Carrolyn,' Robbert says with a hint of exasperation. 'Nothing to worry about.'

'Nothing? I saw the table. That's hardly nothing.'

'It's nothing I didn't see in my hunting days.'

'I hope you went nowhere near the birds. Who knows what diseases and pests they carry?'

'As it happens, I felt that my hunting background could be useful in the investigation and I offered Yannia–' Robbert nods to me, 'my aid.'

Carrolyn barely glances at me, her hand still clutching Robbert's shoulder. 'But what about your health?'

'There's nothing wrong with my health. I'm paralysed, not made of glass.'

Frustration and anguish flicker across Carrolyn's face, but she recovers and smiles. 'If you say so, Robbert. You know where to find me if you need anything.'

'Actually, there is something you can help me with,' he says, checking his watch. 'Could you fetch me a small lump of cheese from the kitchen? I need to give Calleigh her midday tablet.'

For a few seconds, it looks like Carrolyn wants to argue, but then she rises and straightens her shoulders. 'Of course.'

Once Carrolyn has left, Robbert flashes me a wry

smile. 'She's my older sister and seems to think that every time I sneeze, I'm about to keel over.'

'Isn't that a sister's job?' I ask, though I have no personal experience to call upon. The closest I have come to having siblings is watching Karrion interact with his young half-sister and half-brothers. As much as he complains about the noise and stepping on toys on his way to the loo, he is fiercely protective of his family.

'I suppose so.'

Robbert stays in the entrance hall, waiting for Carrolyn, while I leave through the front doors and descend the stone steps. Once I have left the gravel drive for the grounds, I dial Karrion's number. When he answers, his voice is drowned by the shouts and screeches in the background.

'Are you attending a riot over owl rights?' I ask in lieu of a greeting.

'Funny. Mum took a last minute weekend shift, and I offered to take the brood to a circus school taster day. There's no way we could afford it, but I figured the owlets will tire themselves out. I didn't factor in the risk of going deaf, though.'

'Circus training? Is that wise?' Images of Karrion's young siblings doing cartwheels across their cramped lounge spring to mind.

'Bird Shamans make great trapeze artists because we like flying through the air, even if it entails hurtling towards the ground.' Karrion swears and then apologises to someone near him. 'Speaking of which, Robin has just fallen face first off the trampoline.'

'Is he okay?' I ask.

There is a pause before Karrion answers. 'He's fine. All

he asked was whether he could do it again because it was awesome.'

'Yep, he's definitely related to you.'

'I know. What confuses me is that we share a mother rather than a father. Mum is so... sensible.'

'In your family, be grateful at least one of you is.'

'I can be sensible,' Karrion says.

'Wasn't it just last week that I explained to you how impractical subdermal spikes were?'

'Yes, but think how cool they would've looked,' he mutters.

'Sure, right up until the point when you caught one in your fishnet shirt and ripped your back open.'

As I walk around the corner of the building, the large windows of the conservatory come to view. Several people dressed in suits or cocktail dresses, all holding flutes of champagne, appear to be crowding around Robbert and Jessika. I ignore them as I stride across the lawn, the chill wind blowing through my thin shirt, but causing no discomfort.

'So, new topic of conversation,' says Karrion. 'Are you dressed in tweed and ready for a fox hunt yet?'

'Don't be absurd. I'd have more in common with the foxes than the hunters.'

'Yes, but now you're brushing shoulders with the upper echelons of Old London's society, you may yet change your mind.'

'I can't see that happening,' I say, and change the subject as I circle an oval koi pond. The bright scales of the fish flash between lily pads in the weak afternoon sun. 'My visit has been interesting, however, as I have an unofficial case.'

'Really?' Excitement is evident in Karrion's voice. There is a clatter in the background, and he mutters an apology.

I meander past stone benches and marble statues while I recount the events of the past hour. My destination is the dove enclosure, but I have taken a circuitous route in case someone in the conservatory is watching.

'Do you want me to join you?' Karrion asks, a little breathless. 'Mum's working until six, but I could catch an evening train out to Sussex.'

'No need. Jessika's fiancé has volunteered to help me.'

'I see.' The disappointment is plain in Karrion's voice.

'Besides, you'll be of more use in Old London.'

'What do you need?' Karrion asks, eager once more.

'Find out everything you can about Jessika Heeley and Robbert Craichton. There's bad blood between Jessika and her ex-husband, Dharren Hardying, but see what else you can uncover, especially relating to Dharren's whereabouts. I also understand that Robbert was in an accident some time ago. Can you find out what happened?'

'Do you have a hunch?'

'Not yet,' I say. 'At the moment, I'm interested in anything that might explain why someone would want to sabotage the wedding.'

'I'll get right on it.'

'Thanks. While you're at it, do some digging on this hotel. The butler claimed their reputation is excellent, but I want to know whether the Internet agrees.'

'Sure thing. I'll call you as soon as I have something.'

'Great. I hope the kids enjoy the circus training.'

'Wren is currently hanging upside down from the monkey bars. Actually, she looks a little precarious. I'd better–'

The call ends abruptly, and I slip the phone in my back pocket, shaking my head. Wren is far more of a daredevil than Karrion, and she is forever leaping off things to improve her ability to fly. So far, that ability has not extended beyond growing skilled at awkward landings. At the rate her desire to fly is increasing, Karrion and his mother will both have only grey feathers before Wren sits her GCSEs.

I reach the dove enclosure and walk around it. The wooden structure is covered in chicken wire, which looks intact all the way around. It is some three metres tall, and I estimate that the birds have thirty square metres of space. I count fifteen birds, though the coops may contain more. None of them look ill or injured. A mesh-covered door has a lock, which appears secure when I tug on it. There are no scratches around the keyhole. Assuming the dead doves came from this enclosure, whoever took them had a key. This narrows down my pool of suspects and confirms what I already thought: at least one member of staff is involved.

Someone calling my name causes me to turn around. Jessika is beckoning from the open conservatory door, and I abandon my inspection of the dove enclosure. Lunch must be served for the second time.

# CHAPTER 3

Robbert has saved me a seat next to him, like he promised. The waiters have worked fast, and there is no sign that anything untoward happened in the room. It is only I who can still smell a hint of blood and intestines over the scents of asparagus, salmon, and cured ham. The upside of being one of the Wild Folk is that the memory of the butchered doves only serves to increase my appetite.

Lunch is a muted affair. Jessika's voice holds an edge of forced cheerfulness as she maintains conversation with the people nearest to us. All along the table, people are speaking in low voices with their neighbours, eyes drawn towards the centre of the table as though the carcasses were still there. Twice Robbert tries to discuss the investigation with me, but both times I steer the conversation to a neutral topic and he gets the message. We make small talk for the rest of the meal, while my eyes rove among the guests, looking for anything out of place. I spot nothing.

People are slow to leave the table after coffee cups and dessert plates have been cleared away. The conversation has all but died down, and I sense an expectant curiosity in the looks flitting from the centre of the table to us, and back. It is only when Robbert wheels himself away from the table and Jessika stands that others make a move. The wedding party has no set schedule for the rest of the afternoon, but many people return to the conservatory in search of more champagne.

'Would you take Calleigh outside for a moment?' Robbert asks Jessika.

'Of course. Is anything the matter?'

'Yannia and I may wish to interview the kitchen staff and I doubt the management will look kindly on my taking a dog to the kitchen, even if she is a trained assistance animal.'

'Good idea,' I say. 'Hopefully the butler will have had a chance to speak to the kitchen staff while we ate.'

Jessika slips a hand through Calleigh's collar and gently pulls her up. The dog whines, looking to Robbert, and he gives her a pat. Thus reassured, Calleigh follows Jessika without further objection.

We find the kitchen in a flurry of activity. Lunch dishes are stacked to one side, waiting to be washed, while the junior staff members are preparing ingredients for the dinner service, though it is hours away. The butler is speaking to two of the waiters who served lunch. When he spots us, he dismisses them with a wave, and approaches us.

'I trust the lunch was to your satisfaction, sir?'

'It was excellent, thank you,' Robbert says. 'Have you had a chance to interview the kitchen staff yet?'

'Some of them. As you can see, everyone is busy at present. But those I have spoken to do not recall seeing anything out of the ordinary and no one is admitting to mutilating doves in the dining room.'

'If you hear anything further, will you let us know?' I ask.

'Naturally,' the butler says. 'Now if you will excuse me, I need to check whether a delivery of fresh lobsters has arrived.'

We take that as our cue to leave the kitchen and return to the dining room. A waiter is gathering the final glasses and cups off the table onto a wide tray. He lifts it in a faint tinkle of glass and disappears through the door to the kitchen.

I check my phone. Karrion has not called, though I didn't expect him to have found any answers in such a short space of time, especially since he is busy looking after his siblings. I wish I had thought to bring my laptop, but it never occurred to me that I might need it during a wedding.

My eyes are drawn to the fireplace. The inside of it is black with soot, suggesting the logs are not just for show. Would the butler mind if I lit a fire? Most likely. But I have other options.

'Does your room have a functioning fireplace?' I ask Robbert.

'Yes, I think it does. Why?'

'Would you mind terribly if I lit a fire?'

'Are you cold?' Robbert asks.

The memory of the Winter Queen's icy lips on my skin sends a shiver down my spine, but it's not a sensation born of cold. Despite December being only a few days away, I'm dressed for milder weather, no longer worried about the effect of the cold on my joints now a Fey ruler has claimed me as hers.

'No, not cold. But it seems wise to ask for another pair

of eyes to watch over the hotel and your guests, especially the bridal suite since you and Jessika may be the targets of the prank.'

Robbert raises an eyebrow. 'Are you invoking a prayer to a Hearth Spirit?'

'Yes.'

'Why resort to such an outdated custom? If we need more people to solve this mystery, why not call your apprentice here from Old London?'

'A Hearth Spirit will see things we mortals cannot.'

'What makes you think one will help you?'

A smile lifts the corner of my mouth. 'I know a guy.'

'All right.' Robbert shrugs. 'Follow me.'

He leads me to a small lift in the corner of the entrance hall. Soft violin music plays from a discreet speaker on our way up. On the first floor, we head down the same corridor that my room is on, but we continue to the far end. Double doors open to what I take to be the bridal suite. A king-sized four poster bed with lace curtains dominates the space. A sofa and two armchairs are clustered near the floor-to-ceiling windows offering a stunning view of the gardens. There are further doors leading from the main room. The air is scented with vanilla and sandalwood. Another scent lingers in the background, but it slips from my thoughts when, beyond the bed, I spot the fireplace.

It's in keeping with the decor of the room and made out of pale grey bricks. Logs are stacked ready, but the fireplace looks as though it's rarely used. I check the flue is open, and spot on the mantelpiece a box of matches bearing the hotel's logo.

Kneeling on the hearth stones, I strike a match and bring it close to curls of dried bark along the birch logs.

The bark shrivels and blackens before catching. The flames spread along the wood. In the full log basket next to the fireplace, I find a few smaller twigs. It is not much of an offering, but it will have to do. I bring the ends of the twigs near the flames and watch them burn until I feel the heat against my fingers.

'Hearth Spirit, the guarding of the fires near and far, watch over this hotel with the greatest of vigilance. We thank you for your protection and the heat you grant through fires such as this.'

As soon as I have finished speaking, the flames rear high and a figure takes shape within the fire. Wishearth's head and torso emerges from the glow, but upon spotting Robbert a few feet away, he opts not to materialise fully.

'You're far from home and keeping strange company,' Wishearth says, curiosity and reserve warring in his voice.

'I told you I was coming to Sussex for a wedding.'

'That explains one, but not the other.'

'Something strange is going on in the hotel. Someone may be trying to sabotage the wedding.'

Now Wishearth rises from the fire fully and sits cross-legged next to me on the hearth stones. One half of his coat and his left sleeve are dangling in the fire, but the flames never touch them.

'Tell me more,' he says.

I fill him in on the gruesome scene in the dining room and mine and Robbert's speculation about the causes behind it. Robbert adds a few comments, but he is otherwise content to let me speak, choosing instead to stare at Wishearth.

When I have finished, Wishearth reaches for where a

pint of Guinness should be and ends up running a hand through his hair instead. He looks at me, eyes dark with concern.

'I have little power here, so far from the hearths of Old London. A few recall the old ways in this county and those who do whisper their prayers to a different Hearth Spirit. But I will do what I can to aid you, Yannia.'

'Thank you.'

His hot fingers close around mine, sending shivers of ice and fire dancing along my spine, before he rises.

'You may not see me, but I will be watching.'

He fades away until nothing remains of his presence but a dissipating cloud of smoke. Yet I sense him within the fire next to me and know he will keep his word.

'When you said you knew a guy,' Robbert says, clearing his throat. 'I didn't think you meant you were on first name terms with a Hearth Spirit.'

'Rule one of being a PI: you're only as strong as your allies.'

The flames flare high behind me, but I ignore Wishearth's delight. Robbert chuckles.

'I'll bear that in mind. What next?'

'Perhaps it's best you return to your guests. Who knows what interesting bits of gossip Jessika has over-heard while we have been up here. Even if she has nothing new for us, she will doubtless wonder where you've disappeared to.'

'She knows I'm in safe hands, but I take your point.'

I turn towards the door, and in doing so, catch a scent of something out of place. Pausing, I tilt my chin back, trying to locate the source. Robbert doesn't notice and wheels himself around. He gasps.

'What's wrong?' I ask, the strange smell forgotten.

Without a word, he points to the long garment bag hanging behind the suite door. Where it once would have been white, the lower half of it is now stained blue and green. Even as we hurry closer, some corner of my mind notices that the carpet beneath the bag is pristine.

'Is that what I think it is?' I ask.

'Jessika's wedding dress.'

I reach to pick up the coat hanger, draping one arm under the lower half of the bag, before looking around at the closed doors.

'We had better do this in the bathroom.'

'This way.'

Robbert leads me to the door at the far end of the room. The enormous bathroom is, like mine, all chrome and marble. There are two bathtubs; one claw-footed metal bath near the centre of the room and a larger one sunk into a dais at the far end. A control panel is within easy reach of the tub, no doubt for various jets and other functions I cannot even imagine. Closer to us, a shower cubicle has five showerheads. A selection of disability aids have been brought in for Robbert.

I lay the garment bag on the steps leading up to the larger bathtub so that we can both examine the dress. When I draw down the zipper, the scent I detected earlier intensifies: a mixture of ink and spell components, taking me back to Gideor Braeman's study and my first big case in Old London. I push aside the memory of the secrets Karrion and I uncovered in that room, and focus on the dress.

It's ivory silk, with lace sleeves and a body of shimmering pearl flowers that widens into a ruffled skirt.

Once, it was beautiful, if a little old-fashioned. Now the dress is beyond salvage.

Ink has been splashed down the front from where the body ends and the skirt begins. The colour of it varies from blue to shimmering green. Robbert reaches his fingers to touch the stained fabric, but I hold him back.

'Don't. The ink is mixed with liquid heart copper. It's permanent. If you touch the ink, it won't come off your fingers.'

'Who would pour a bottle of an expensive spell ingredient on a wedding dress?'

'Someone who wanted to make sure Jessika wouldn't wear it on Sunday. No spell, no matter how powerful, can remove all traces of the ink. The dress is ruined.'

'She's going to be devastated.' Robbert glances over his shoulder, perhaps worried that speaking her name will summon her. 'How am I going to tell her? There's no time to find another dress before Sunday.'

'It will be poor consolation to Jessika, but we now know whoever is behind these incidents *is* trying to sabotage the wedding. If they wanted to stain the reputation of the hotel, they would concentrate on the public areas of the building.'

I rise and pluck a tissue from a box on the counter. Rolling it into a tight wad between my hands, I press one end against the hem of the dress. It comes back stained green.

'The ink is still wet. My guess is that whoever ruined the dress did so while we were having lunch.'

'That eliminates all the wedding guests.'

'Not necessarily.' I pace away to throw the tissue in the bin. 'The only way to access this suite is with a key card. Am I right to assume only you and Jessika have copies?'

'Yes.'

'Then the culprit will have needed help from a staff member, just like they did with the doves. What better way to create an alibi than to be eating lunch in full view of your guests while something else occurs in a different part of the hotel?'

'This is getting serious,' Robbert says, rubbing his forehead. 'It's one thing to pull a gruesome prank in the public areas of the hotel, quite another to break into our room.'

'I agree. It would be worth checking whether anything has been stolen. Can you do that while I find Jessika? The sooner we tell her about this, the better.'

'You're right.'

We leave the dress laid out on the steps of the tub and shut the door behind us. On my way to the door, I check the windows for an alternative way in. Although we are on the first floor, the distance to the ground is little more than an interesting challenge for a thief, especially one possessing magic.

Perhaps I ought to check what Fria is up to this weekend?

The windows are all locked. What convinces me of the impossibility of gaining access to the room through them are the safety catches that prevent the windows from being opened more than four inches. Even a magical thief needs space to slip inside. Whoever ruined the dress gained entrance through the door.

# CHAPTER 4

Downstairs, I find Jessika talking to her mother and an elderly couple. From their expensive clothes and the perpetual sneers on their faces, I take them to be members of the Mage aristocracy. My steps slow down, an automatic reaction to the implied hierarchy of our world. As soon as I catch myself doing so, I straighten my shoulders and quicken my pace.

'Jessika,' I say, clearing my throat. 'Might I borrow you for a moment, please?'

Jessika's mother turns, a cold gaze flickering up and down. Once again, I am found unsuitable. I shove my hands into my jeans pockets to hide my palms.

'We didn't order drinks,' she says, and turns her back to me without waiting for a response.

'Just as well I didn't bring any.' I fight to keep my voice level. 'Jessika, Robbert and I need you.'

'Lord and Lady Warrengton; Mother; will you excuse me,' Jessika says.

'Why are the grounds maintenance staff addressing your daughter with such familiarity?' Lord Warrengton asks Jessika's mother.

'She's one of them,' Jessika's mother lowers her voice, but keeps her words perfectly audible, 'you know, the savages from the north.'

'Oh.'

Both Lord and Lady Warrengton stare at me with open curiosity, taking in my casual clothes and the smudges of mud clinging to my shoes after my trip to the dove cage. Heat floods my cheeks under such unabashed scrutiny. All that separates me from a zoo animal is the lack of bars.

'Come, Yannia.'

Jessika takes my hand and draws me away. Calleigh, who had been lying at Jessika's feet, rises stiffly and follows us. As we leave, I catch Lady Warrengton asking Jessika's mother whether I am the family's charity case. Fortunately we are out of earshot of even my enhanced hearing before any reply is forthcoming. I am briefly grateful Karrion is not here. His piercings and goth clothes would attract equal comments and his temper is even quicker to flare than mine.

'Thanks for the rescue,' Jessika whispers as we ascend the stairs. 'I was starting to feel desperate. Had I not left my phone in my room, I would have texted you to stage a wedding crisis so I could have an excuse to leave.'

'It's fine,' I say, trying to bring my emotions under control.

It has been some time since I felt like an outsider among spell casters. I thought I had found myself a place in Old London, had gained acceptance and perhaps even approval among my magical peers. But today has been a reminder that I am only accepted among the lower classes, the outcasts, and those beyond the traditional tiers of hierarchy. Lord Ellensthorne may owe me his life, but that doesn't mean he views me as an equal.

'Are you okay?' Jessika asks.

'Robbert and I have something to show you.'

She tries to ask further questions, but I remain silent until we reach the bridal suite. Robbert is waiting near the door, twisting his hands on his lap. As soon as the door opens wide enough to admit us, Calleigh trots forward and takes her place next to Robbert's chair. He strokes her head with one hand while the other dips into his suit pocket for a dog biscuit. His eyes remain locked on the dog a moment too long.

'What's going on?' Jessika asks, fear colouring her voice.

'There has been another incident,' he says, and reaches to grasp Jessika's hand. 'I'm so sorry, my dear.'

'What's going on?' Jessika asks again.

'It's your wedding dress.'

'No.' She takes a step back. 'What's happened to it?'

Rather than explain, Robbert turns around and wheels to the bathroom door. He pushes it open and flicks on the light. Jessika hovers by the threshold, eyes fixed on him, before stepping into the bathroom. A moan signals the moment she spots the dress.

I walk to the desk and dial the number for reception. When someone answers, I ask them to send the butler up to the bridal suite.

When I can delay witnessing Jessika's reaction no longer, I walk to the bathroom door. Jessika is kneeling on the tiled floor next to the dress, shaking her head as she surveys the stained fabric. Glancing over her shoulder, she notices me.

'Would you,' she begins to speak and has to clear her throat, 'would you hold it up for me?'

'Of course.'

I stand at the top step and ease the edges of the coat hanger out of the garment bag. Careful to keep the bag under the dress in case ink drips from the hem and stains the tiles, I lift the dress.

The ink has soaked through to the back. Stained silk ribbons hang from the bodice and the pearl buttons look like they have been dulled by age and mould. Jessika brings a hand to cover her mouth, and her eyes fill with tears.

'It's all ruined,' she whispers.

'I'm so sorry,' Robbert says, lacing the fingers of her free hand with his. 'We'll find a way to make this right.'

'We can't find another dress with less than two days' notice.'

'Even if you walk down the aisle in your pyjamas, you'll be the most beautiful bride ever seen,' Robbert says.

Jessika offers him a watery smile, but her eyes stray back to the wedding dress. Disappointment is written across her face. I cannot blame her. Which girl doesn't dream of the perfect dress for the perfect day? At least, which Mage girl from an aristocratic family? Things are different for the likes of me, born to the wild tribes of the north, where tradition matters more than individual choice and I have no say over my mate or the date of my mating. Jessika will never know how lucky she is, but telling her so will not fix the problem we are facing.

My arms ache. I am about to lower the dress when the light reflecting off the fabric catches my eye. The colour of the ink is uneven in places. I frown. Is it a trick of the light or are there symbols beneath the stains? I shift the dress first one way and then the other to find the best angle for the light. There. Now I am certain I can make out several symbols painted onto the fabric. They were made using the same heart copper ink, but because they were painted first, the ink is a slightly darker shade of metallic green. Shifting my grip on the dress, I reach into my back pocket for my phone and snap a couple of photos of the symbols.

'Did you find something?' Robbert asks.

'I think so.' I lower the dress onto the bag, heedless of it landing in a heap. 'Do these look familiar?'

Robbert takes the phone I offer him and flicks through the photos. He zooms in and out, studying each symbol with care.

'I think they are Mage symbols,' he says at last. 'But it's difficult to tell, given how unclear they are.'

'If they're Mage symbols, what are they used for?' I ask.

'Spells, rituals, curses. Take your pick.'

'Curses?' Jessika's voice rises. 'Are you saying someone cursed my wedding dress?'

'It could be something as simple as wanting the dress to be beyond salvage,' Robbert says, taking her hand in his.

I want to remind him that the ink has already achieved that goal, but his eyes tighten in warning. It takes a matter of moments to send the images to Karrion with a request to find out what they are for. Tinker Thaylor should know, and a visit to One Magic Change will soothe Karrion's ruffled feathers for having to stay in the sidelines for this investigation.

A discreet tap at the door signals the arrival of the butler. Robbert leads Jessika out of the bathroom while I explain the situation. He turns pale at the news of a ruined dress and paler still when he sees the damage.

'How can this be?' he mumbles to no one in particular.

'Is there a way to find out when anyone has used a key card to enter this room, or does your system only record the most recent entry?'

'We keep track of all key card activity,' he says, struggling to keep his attention away from the dress.

'Great. In that case, we need to know when people have entered this room today.'

'Of course. I will obtain that information for you presently. Shall I also dispose of the dress?'

'Please. I think keeping it here will only upset Jessika further. But be careful. The ink is magical and if any transfers onto you, it will be permanent.'

He swallows and gathers the dress in the bag with extreme reluctance. Once it has been safely zipped, he carries it out of the room. I turn to follow, when something on the floor catches my eye and I bend down to inspect it. It is a downy grey feather, identical to the one I found downstairs earlier. The colour blends in with the tiled floor, and I have no way of telling how long it has been here. Is it a coincidence, or something more? I tuck it into my pocket next to the first feather.

I follow the butler downstairs. He instructs the receptionist to print me a list of key card entries for the bridal suite while he takes away the wedding dress. There are only three entries on the list: first thing that morning, an hour and a half ago, and some thirty minutes ago. The first will have been when Jessika and Robbert checked in, the last when Robbert took me to speak to Wishearth.

That leaves the one in the middle. It was right when we were having lunch.

As I suspected, a member of staff is involved, thereby giving the guest behind these incidents an alibi. If a guest is involved at all. It is possible we are dealing with someone outside the wedding party. Dharren is the obvious suspect, but could he truly be this intent upon ruining his ex-wife's second chance at happiness?

My phone rings and an image of a pigeon flashes across the screen. I hurry outside, choosing the privacy of the garden over the danger of being overheard inside. The Winter Queen's curse goes some way towards insulating me from the cold, so the chill holds little menace for me. When I answer my phone, the first thing I hear are Karrion's siblings in the background as they try to entice a magpie onto their palms.

'I feel like you're giving me homework,' Karrion says without bothering with a greeting. 'Will you be paying me overtime? Come to think of it, shouldn't we set working hours for your poor apprentice at some point? I haven't had a day off in ages.'

'How is it that I remember a whole week of us lounging on my bed eating pizza and listening to old radio shows while I couldn't use my hands? We haven't had a proper case since we helped Lady Bergamon, and your wages have been paid by none other than your favourite politician, Lord Ellensthorne.'

Karrion makes a gagging sound. 'Must you always ruin everything?'

'That is my job as your boss.'

In truth, I regret making the joke. We have not spoken about what happened on the night Baneacre attacked Lord

Ellensthorne and I watched Karrion almost kill himself to bring back a flock of dead birds. It is a sore between us, a wound that has not yet scabbed over, and I fear it will be a long while before the scar tissue has faded to the same silvery colour as those across my palms. I flex the hand not holding the phone and feel the skin catch and pull in unfamiliar ways. The pain is almost gone, but it has left behind a memory of the weeks my wounds took to heal. Without Lady Bergamon's aid, I doubt I would have even a fraction of the use of my hands I once took for granted.

'You're lucky I was on my way home with the brood. I can make a detour to One Magic Change. The owlets haven't stopped pestering me for some spell crackers since I mentioned needing to go there.'

'Can you imagine Wren in Tinker Thaylor's work-shop?' I ask with a grin.

'I can and I'm not that stupid or suicidal. Thaylor would skin me if the goslings break something. A friend of mine, Amenda, runs one of the stalls downstairs. I'll ask her to keep an eye on the cygnets while I run upstairs.'

'No fair,' says Wren in the background. 'I want to fly upstairs too.'

'So that's a no to spell crackers, then?'

The children fall silent, and Karrion sighs.

'I know bribery is bad, but sometimes it's the only feather in my quiver. Anyway, Thaylor should be able to interpret those symbols for us.'

'Thanks, Karrion. Let me know when you have something to report.'

'You didn't think I only called to complain did you?' he asks with a laugh.

'Go on then, what have you found out?'

Karrion pauses to herd his siblings into a bus and up to the top floor. When he speaks, he keeps his voice low.

'I started with Jessika's husband-to-be. Finding the details of the accident wasn't difficult at all. The media were all over it at the time, given that he's from an influential Mage family. They don't have any of the South Mage seats on the High Council at the moment, but there are various rumours online that if Robbert takes a greater interest in politics in the future, he's almost guaranteed a place on the Council.'

'At least he will be one person we won't have to vet. I can confirm here and now that he's definitely not a Leech.'

'But we'll still charge Lord Ellensthorne for this, right?' asks Karrion.

'Of course. Carry on.'

'So Robbert used to be married to someone called Sussannah and they had twin daughters. From what I can tell, theirs was a perfect happy family, if those ever exist in real life. Fifteen years ago, they went skiing in France over Easter. It was pretty warm that spring and the melting snows triggered an avalanche. The only reason the rescuers found Robbert before he suffocated was that one of his ski poles stuck out of the snow when he was buried. He'd been pretty bashed up, which damaged his spine, and having to be dug out of the snow only worsened the damage. Despite the best healers money can buy and extensive physiotherapy, he never regained the use of his legs.'

Here is the wall that rises before us all, magical or human: there are some hurts, some diseases even magic cannot cure. We are not all powerful, nor do we have mastery over death. Even the most powerful among us will bleed and die just like humans.

'What about Sussannah and the daughters?'

'They were buried so deep it was weeks before their bodies were found.'

'Poor Robbert.'

The words are inadequate, but I cannot think of another way to express my sorrow for the tragedy in the distant past.

'It must have been horrible for him,' says Karrion, 'stuck in hospital while the locals searched for the bodies of his family. He disappeared from the public eye for years after the funeral. When he returned, it was clear that he would never walk again and that he'd made his peace with it. But there was never so much as a hint of a romance with anyone, until his engagement to Jessika was announced.'

'She told me they met in a supermarket,' I say. 'He asked her to reach for something on a high shelf for him and they started chatting. A cup of coffee turned into dinner, which turned into them talking all night. It was a coincidence that he had chosen to assert his independence by going shopping alone the same day as she had refused to let the housekeeper get her groceries. A year on, they're about to get married.'

'So long as the wedding isn't called off because of these pranks. We'd better solve this case fast.'

I smile at his choice of words. Even though he is not physically here, he is invested in the mystery and as keen to help people as always. In this, at least, he hasn't changed.

'My thoughts exactly,' I say. 'But the symbols painted onto the wedding dress concern me. What if they're a hint of something far more sinister than a series of pranks to spoil the weekend's celebrations?'

'Tinker Thaylor will be able to figure that out for us. If someone put a curse on the dress, she should know how to break it.'

If it can be broken. I leave the thought unspoken. Karrion and I have faced far worse and solved the cases. Like him, I must believe that we can do so again.

A bell chimes in the background, and Karrion calls 'Let's go!' to his siblings.

'We're at One Magic Change. I'll call you back as soon as I have news.'

'Thanks. You'll look into Dharren as well, won't you? And see what you can find out about Jessika's family. There may be recent scandals I've missed.'

'Of course. I'll tell Thaylor you said hi.'

We end the call. A deep longing for Old London sweeps over me, surprising me with its intensity. The hotel grounds are surrounded by woods, yet I miss the city. Old London has become my home and I have shed blood to keep it safe. Without noticing, I've begun to view it as mine more than the unspoilt lands of the north. Those are the conclave's, the Elderman's, Dearon's, not mine. Yet there will come a time when all of that will change. One day I must have a claim over those lands, call them mine, though my place there will always be a rung lower than Dearon's. He may be my promised mate, but we will never be equals.

The scents of the dusk air turn bitter in my nose. I turn back to the hotel and climb the stone steps to the front door. I glance over my shoulder. A dark line of trees on the far end of the lawn is a promise of wilderness. But I drove through them on my way here, saw the farmlands, the country manors, the villages, and the sports clubs. It is an empty promise. I go back inside.

# CHAPTER 5

A clatter of heels on the marble floor draws my thoughts back to the present. Three women, whom Jessika pointed out to me over lunch as her bridal party, rush to Robbert, who has just wheeled himself out of the lift. They speak in hushed tones that convey shock and concern, before crowding into the lift, eyes already glancing up as they wait for the doors to close. Robbert spots me, and we meet at the centre of the entrance hall.

'How is Jessika?' I ask.

'A little calmer, but still understandably upset. I asked the bridesmaids to go upstairs to help her figure out what to do about a new dress.'

'Perhaps one of them will have a bright idea.'

'It's better than my suggestion that she will look stunning even in her pyjamas.'

'No doubt she'll appreciate it in time,' I say.

'Shall we have coffee?' Robbert motions towards the bar area.

'Good idea.'

We find a table by the French windows, away from the other guests, and I push one of the heavy armchairs away to make room for Robbert's wheelchair. A waiter comes over, and we order two cups of coffee. With a sigh, Calleigh settles down next to Robbert's chair.

'Robbert,' comes a voice from behind us, 'there you are. I've been looking everywhere for you.'

Carrolyn, Robbert's sister, hurries to our table. Her eyes roam over Robbert with an intensity that goes beyond a sister's concern. Why is she so worried?

'I haven't been hiding,' he says, patting her hand. 'Jessika needed me upstairs.'

'Are you well?'

'I'm fine. So is Jessika, thank you for asking.'

Carrolyn purses her lips as she huffs. 'Why wouldn't she be? In two days, you will be married.'

Despite her words, Carrolyn doesn't seem happy about the wedding. Does she not think Jessika good enough for Robbert? Is it the age difference? I will have to ask Karrion to see what he can find out about her.

'Someone appears to be sabotaging our wedding weekend, so it's no wonder Jessika is upset.'

'Has something else happened?'

'Someone poured magical ink over Jessika's wedding dress.'

I shoot a warning glance in Robbert's direction. Carrolyn may be his sister, but I would prefer it if we kept the details of the vandalism to a minimum.

'Who would do such a thing?' Carrolyn asks, her hands clasped together in front of her.

'That's what we're trying to figure out,' Robbert says, casting a meaningful look in my direction.

'And I'm in the way.' Carrolyn nods. 'I know when I'm not wanted. I'll leave you to it.'

'Don't be like that,' Robbert says, but she has already turned on her heels and is striding away.

Robbert watches her go and rubs his face. 'She means

well, but there are times when her melodrama becomes tedious.'

'No family is perfect.'

'Not even yours?'

I laugh, and fight to keep bitterness from my voice. 'Hardly.'

He looks like he wants to ask me to explain, but a waiter arrives with our coffees and the moment passes.

While we stir our drinks, I tell him what I discovered about access to their hotel suite. His expression darkens, and when he lifts the cup to his lips, his hand is shaking.

'So whoever is behind all this can walk into our room at any point, day or night?'

'I'm afraid so.'

'How will I keep Jessika safe if we are attacked during the night?' Robbert sets his cup down on the saucer, and some of the coffee spills over the rim. 'I can't exactly stand between them and shield her with my body.'

'You have your magic,' I say, choosing my words with care for fear of offending him. 'I have no doubt that you could defend Jessika against any number of attackers. But as a precaution, I will ask Wishearth to keep an eye out for intruders and to give you advance warning should anyone try to enter your suite during the night.'

'Thank you,' Robbert says, but his frown only deepens. 'I never knew what it meant to be helpless before the accident. In fact, I led my life with the absolute certainty that I could accomplish anything I wanted to, that none of my dreams were beyond my capabilities. Now I need help with washing and dressing myself.'

'The past couple of months have taught me that being strong doesn't mean not needing help, but rather knowing when to ask for it.'

He smiles, but I know my words are of little comfort. There are other ways for him to regain his sense of security and he seems to agree with me.

'I'll feel better once we have solved this case,' he says.

'Me too. My apprentice is looking into the symbols painted onto the wedding dress. I've also asked him to see if he can track down Jessika's ex-husband.'

'Do you think Dharren is behind all this?'

'I'm not sure. He seems like the obvious choice, though perhaps he is too obvious. Are there any guests present who wouldn't want to see you and Jessika married?'

Robbert thinks.

'Carrolyn has been... hesitant to welcome Jessika into the family. She thinks Jessika is too young for me or I too old for her. But I cannot imagine her ever going so far as to try to sabotage the wedding. Also, she fainted when her cat brought a bird into the house and gutted it on the carpet. So I cannot see her deciding to arrange butchered doves in a macabre shape.'

This ties in with my own thoughts on Carrolyn. She may be an overprotective older sister, but I sense no true malice towards Jessika.

'Anyone else?'

'Not to my knowledge. Neither of us have invited past lovers, not that we have many of those. We are among friends here, or so I thought.'

I hesitate a moment before asking my next question. 'What about any of your first wife's family or friends? Might they be angry that you are remarrying?'

'No. I spoke to Sussannah's parents before I proposed to Jessika. They gave me their blessing. It has been years since Sussannah and our girls passed away, and I never thought I'd find someone else. Sussannah's father told me they were happy for me. We will always be bound by the tragedy, but they want me to move on. I believe Sussannah would, too.'

'That narrows our likely suspect pool to Dharren and no one else.'

'I'll keep thinking. Perhaps I'll come up with another name. But to be honest, we wouldn't have invited anyone who didn't want to be here or who objected to the wedding.'

From the corner of my eye, I notice a man walk into the bar area and make a beeline for our table. He taps Robbert on the shoulder.

'Are you ready, mate? We need to leave in fifteen minutes.'

Robbert twists in his chair and points to the man standing next to him. 'Yannia, this is my best man, Jaike. Jaike, this is Yannia.'

We shake hands.

'Jaike has organised something of a stag do for me, given that we will all be in the same place this weekend. A local archery club has converted their shooting range for us to do spell-casting practice on.'

'We have a whole host of targets for speed, distance and accuracy,' Jaike says with a grin. 'Wait till you see how we've modified them.'

'Perhaps we should cancel?' Robbert aims his question at me. 'Given what's happened today, I'm not sure it will be wise for me to leave the hotel.'

'Not at all. There's little we can do while we are waiting for information from my apprentice. Enjoy your night off.'

'Are you certain?'

'One of the biggest secrets in my profession is that we do our best work when we make time for fun things in our lives.'

'All right then,' Robbert says with a laugh.

Jaike heads back towards the door, but Robbert hesitates. I finish my coffee as I stand up.

'Don't worry,' I say. 'Wishearth and I will keep an eye on things while you're away.'

This seems to reassure him, and he wheels after Jaike.

I speak to the waiter to ask that the coffees are charged to my room, and check my phone. No messages from Karrion. Perhaps Tinker Thaylor has distracted him with talk of metal wings so that he may learn to fly. More likely is that his siblings have escaped their temporary babysitter and are on the loose in One Magic Change. It is a terrifying thought, and I am glad I'm not there to try to catch them.

I meander to the reception hall, only to run into Jessika. She has refreshed her make-up and has changed into a silver dress, and upon spotting me, she smiles.

'There you are. Robbert mentioned you were at the bar.'

'We had coffee while we discussed the case,' I say.

Her expression falters briefly, but she shakes her head. 'My maid of honour insists that I have a night off. We're going dancing at a nightclub not far from here. The whole bridal party, minus my mother, is coming. Would you like to join us?'

The possibility of spending the evening in a darkened room surrounded by beautiful strangers is tempting. I could lose myself in the music, find a woman to dance with, allow alcohol to burn away the questions nagging at the back of my mind. For a few hours, I could be a young woman at a nightclub rather than Yannia Wilde, Private Investigator. But as tempting as the invitation is, I need to stay focused on the case.

'I think it's best if I stay here. Wishearth and I will keep an eye on things. That way you and Robbert can go off to your respective parties and enjoy yourselves without having to worry about the wedding.'

'Are you sure?'

'Positive. But do you happen to have a laptop or a tablet in your room that I could borrow? I didn't think to bring mine, and there is some research I'd like to do this evening.'

'Of course. Will you come and pick it up now?'

'If that suits you?'

'Certainly.'

Together we walk up the stairs. When we reach the bridal suite, we find one of the hotel staff fumbling with a key card, a tower of pillows balancing on one arm.

'Here, let me,' Jessika says and unlocks the door.

The young woman follows us in and moves all the pillows on the bed away and replaces them with those she brought with her. As a final touch, she takes two more pillows from the walk-in wardrobe and leaves with all of them.

'Will this be okay?'

Jessika's question interrupts my thoughts, and I turn to find her offering me a laptop bag. In addition to a laptop, it contains a charger, a mouse, and a small keyboard.

'It's perfect, thank you.'

'Bring it back whenever you're done with it. I doubt Robbert will have much time for checking his emails this weekend, and he can always use my tablet. The Wi-Fi password is in your welcome pack.'

'Thanks. I hope you have a fun evening.'

Jessika smiles at me and turns to look through her travel jewellery case. I stare at it, trying to recall whether it sat on the side table when I was in this room earlier. Too many things occupied my mind, so I can't remember.

'Jessika, do you keep your jewellery in the safe?'

She looks up, surprised by the question. 'No, I don't. Do you think I should?'

'Under normal circumstances, I wouldn't worry about it. But as things stand, yes, it's a good idea.'

'All right. Once I've picked out what I'm going to wear for the evening, I'll lock the rest away.'

'Good,' I say. 'See you at breakfast.'

I leave her to her preparations, but as I walk down the corridor, I think it strange that the jewellery had not been touched. Had her wedding dress been ruined by an unscrupulous outsider or even a member of the staff, a case full of expensive jewellery must have been a great temptation. Why was nothing taken? It's as though the mystery person is both prepared to destroy a wedding dress, but honest enough not to help themselves to jewellery. Where is the logic in that?

# CHAPTER 6

Once I reach my room, I set the laptop bag on the table. While the laptop boots, I meander to the bed and pick up one of the pillows. It's soft and plump. My hand leaves a deep impression in the middle. Borrowing the nose of a hedgehog snoozing in a pile of leaves in the garden, I lift the pillow to my face and inhale. Goose down. I check the other pillows as well as the spares in the cupboard. They are all filled with down.

What does it mean? A theory is beginning to form at the back of my mind, but it is too nebulous to make sense as yet. Perhaps Karrion will be able to shed some light on this mystery.

I connect the laptop to the hotel's Wi-Fi and open a browser. My hands hover over the keyboard while I try to figure out where to begin. The silvery scars covering my palms itch. I scratch at them absently, and a twinge of pain reminds me of burning leather gloves, blackening Fey flesh, and the terrible weight of a Fey Lord's will asserting itself over mine.

To escape the memories, I rise and pace to the fireplace. I stack logs onto blackened bricks and for the second time that day, make an offering to Wishearth.

'Hearth Spirit, the guardian of all hearths, thank you

for your protection through these hours of darkness. May everyone be safe within these walls.'

'Is it just this room you're talking about or the whole hotel?' asks a smoky voice from amidst the flames.

'The hotel,' I say as I rise, my knees groaning in protest.

'You should be more specific. Implication doesn't work in prayers.'

'Do you want me to start again and make an offering to a different Hearth Spirit?'

Wishearth rises from the flames, taking form on the hearth stones. 'There's no need to get snippy.'

'I'm sorry. It's been a weird day.'

'Tell me.'

He draws me to the sofa facing the fireplace. We sit side by side, our knees touching as we face one another. His warmth seeps into my leg and along my bones until all of me is suffused in soothing heat. Between that and the smell of wood smoke curling around me, I relax as I relay the events of the evening.

'You will have your work cut out for you if you have to investigate each guest for a possible motive for ruining the wedding,' Wishearth says when I have finished.

'I know. Even with Karrion and Robbert helping me, I doubt we can do it in less than two days. More than that, I worry that if we divert our attention to what could be a wild Shaman chase, we'll leave an opening for further damage.'

'You think whoever is behind these pranks will strike again?'

'Why wouldn't they? If the aim is to ruin the wedding, they haven't achieved that yet. The doves unsettled the guests, but none left. And while the loss of the dress caused Jessika a great deal of distress, she will find something else to wear for Sunday. Robbert's admiration will make her feel beautiful regardless of whether she wears a proper wedding dress or not.'

'You seem certain of that.'

'I've seen the way he looks at her,' I say, speaking to my knees. A sparkle of fireflies has appeared in my stomach, and for some reason, I dare not look at Wishearth. 'If that's not love, I don't know what is.'

'Love comes in many guises.'

It may be my imagination, but Wishearth's voice sounds husky. A shiver runs through me, as I wonder how we veered away from the case and the threat to Jessika and Robbert's wedding.

'Are you cold?' he asks.

'A little,' I say, though it's a lie. Being cold means something different now I've been marked by the Winter Queen. But explaining why I am shivering is too complicated.

Wishearth takes my hands in his and sends heat deep into my limbs. When I at last force my eyes to meet his, I find them engulfed by flames. They cast dancing shadows over his cheekbones, highlighting the long strands of his hair orange. I cannot recall ever seeing him look more beautiful. We stare at each other, frozen in a cocoon of heat, and his fingers slide over the insides of my wrists.

I find myself leaning forward, my mouth open to speak, though I have no idea what to say. All words have faded away, leaving behind only this moment and Wishearth's presence occupying all my senses. He shifts forward, as if to meet me halfway, when a discordant noise makes me jump.

It takes me a few seconds to realise my phone is ringing and a few more to work out that in order to answer it, I will have to let go of Wishearth's hand. I pull mine back, but in doing so, my fingertips skim over his palms and the flames in his eyes flare before fading away.

'Hi, Karrion,' I say, fighting to keep a tremor from my voice.

'Is this a bad time?' he asks, ever sensitive to my moods.

'No, it's fine. I was just telling Wishearth about the case.'

'Wishearth is there?'

There is an unmistakable note of caution in Karrion's voice, and next to me, Wishearth grins. I roll my eyes at him. Although Wishearth can clearly hear Karrion, I switch the phone onto speaker and lay it on the table.

'I asked for his help in keeping Jessika and Robbert safe,' I manage to say without laughing.

'Right. Yeah, that makes sense.'

'What have you found out?'

'Thaylor sends her regards. She says you owe her a pair of leather gloves.'

'She should put them on my tab. I must have one by now.'

'Try as you may, you can't seem to stay out of trouble when it comes to Mages.'

I have little desire to go over old ground or dwell on the memory of Ilana telling me I failed her. My track record has been far from spotless and each of those failures weighs heavily on my conscience.

'Did she recognise the symbols?' I ask.

'Yes, though she couldn't make them all out because of the ink that had been poured over them. But she said they were part of an East Mage ritual.'

'For what?'

'That's what she wasn't sure about. Thaylor said it could either be a blessing for a happy marriage or a curse dooming the husband and wife to a life of misery and loss. Weirdly, the two are fairly similar at their core.'

'Doesn't that tie in with the old adage about love and hate being perfect for each other,' Wishearth says.

Karrion huffs. 'I don't think it works quite like that, but point taken.'

'Given that the wedding dress was destroyed, I don't think it's a great leap to assume that in this case, the symbols were used to try to doom the marriage.'

'I agree,' Karrion says. 'Thaylor thought that ruining the dress may even have been a part of the ritual. It is more effective if something vital to the ceremony is sacrificed while the spell is cast.'

'That's not good. I'm not sure whether I should tell that to Jessika and Robbert.'

'Why?' asks Karrion.

'Let's say they find out their marriage is cursed before they've even spoken their vows, but they decide to proceed anyway. Every time they have an argument or they wonder if they made the right choice, the curse will come up. It will be the cause and the consequence of all negativity between them.'

'Thus becoming a self-fulfilling prophecy,' says Wishearth. 'The marriage is cursed so it fails, and it fails because it was cursed and they never had a chance.'

'Exactly.'

'Are you going to lie to them?' Karrion asks.

'Possibly by omission,' I say. 'Thaylor wasn't sure and at this point in the investigation, making choices based on incomplete information is unwise.'

'Did she say whether it's possible to break the curse before Jessika and Robbert get married?' Wishearth asks.

I smile at him, impressed by the question. Wishearth seems invested, as caught up in the mystery as Karrion and I. Something is shifting in the dynamics of my life, and it leaves me unsure of my balance.

'Thaylor said there's a way to reverse most spells, but she couldn't remember how to do so with this one. She's looking into it and promised to call me tomorrow.'

'Good. I really appreciate your help on this, Karrion.'

'Hey, what are apprentices for if not doing all the legwork?' He laughs, and although I only saw him yesterday, I find myself missing his easy grin and unwavering optimism. At least he is helping me from afar.

'I'll bear that in mind when you next complain about legwork. Keep digging and see what you can find out about the hotel. I'll call you tomorrow morning if there are any more developments here.'

'Sure thing. If you do need me to come there, let me know.'

We say our goodbyes, and I end the call. As I slip the phone into my pocket, I find Wishearth watching me with a smile.

'What?' I ask.

'When you're fully involved in a mystery, you have a tiny crease beneath your lower lip. It makes you look both introspective and petulant at the same time.'

'Shut up,' I say, throwing a sofa cushion at him to hide the heat rising in my cheeks.

His husky chuckle follows me to the desk, where I pick up the laptop. When I come back to the sofa, he has returned the cushion to its proper place. I claim a corner spot, drawing my feet up and balancing the laptop on my knees.

'Am I supposed to just sit here and watch you work?' Wishearth asks, sparks flaring in his eyes. 'Is that what you pay Karrion for?'

'Pretty much, though his contract stipulates that he needs to look impressed by my insights.'

'I'm not sure I can stretch to that. Is bemused surprise enough?'

With a huff of mock irritation, I fumble for the cushion behind me, but it's wedged between the hand rest and my back.

'I can see why you spend your days drinking rather than solving crimes,' I say, and laugh at Wishearth's spluttered objection.

'Speaking of drinking, I'll be right back.'

He fades into a cloud of smoke before I have a chance to reply. His scent lingers in the room; a promise of a return. No longer surprised by his mercurial ways, I turn my attention to the laptop and begin typing. When a tumbler of brandy appears in my field of vision moments later, I jump and the edge of the laptop almost knocks the drink out of his hand.

'Do you ever knock?' I ask, trying to recover from the fear of brandy spilling over the keyboard.

'Why would I, when you've extended me the welcome of your hearth and home?'

'What if I'd decided to get changed or take a shower?'

'Would it be any different to any of the times when you've undressed in front of the fireplace?'

I take the tumbler from him, grateful to have something to focus my gaze on. The brandy burns in my throat, but I am certain my cheeks are far hotter than the strongest of alcohols. More than once I have wondered whether he's watched me discarding my clothes and slipping under the covers in front of the fire. The thought of his eyes on me should leave me feeling violated, but instead it causes a knot to coil and twist in my stomach. For he is right: Wishearth will come to my home only when I invite him through the offerings and prayers.

Heedless of my embarrassment, he returns to his spot on the sofa and sets a pint of Guinness on the coffee table. His hands free, he reaches for my calves and tugs my legs forward until they are draped across his lap. Heat envelops them, easing the ache that is always present.

'This will help with the pain,' he says, casting a sideways glance at me. This time, there is no humour in them, only something darker and more serious.

'Thanks.'

There is more I'd like to say, just like I would like to reach out and lay my hand on his. But I dare not for fear of what might happen next. We have stepped into uncharted terrain, and I am unsure of my footing.

Perhaps he senses my hesitation, for he leans forward to take his pint and raises it in salute.

'Cheers,' I say, and take another sip of my brandy.

'I charged these to your room, by the way,' Wishearth says.

'And I assumed you went all the way back to the Open Hearth to fetch us drinks.'

'It's too far. Since you called me away from Old London, I shall remain here for the duration of your visit.'

'I'm sorry,' I say, immediately concerned that my asking for help here has caused offence.

'No need to be. I can still hear the other prayers in Old London, I simply won't accept them in person. It is nice to have a change of scenery, especially as I'm no longer a regular visitor to a small Wild Folk conclave in the Northern country.'

This is not the first time Wishearth has hinted that he has known me far longer than I have lived in Old London, but I have never persuaded him to give me a straight answer on the matter. I find it comforting to know, or at least to suspect, that a small piece of my childhood is by my side every day as I try to make sense of life in the city. It gives me hope that when I must return to the conclave and take my place at Dearon's side, I may not lose every connection I have forged in Old London.

Wishearth shifts so he is partly facing me and rests his pint on the back of the sofa. He seems content to watch me while I go through the search results for my first keywords. Sometime later, I become aware of his free hand coming to rest on my ankle. His thumb rubs slow circles on my exposed skin, sending sparks of heat up my leg. The warmth seems to pool in my lower belly, but I force my focus to remain on the computer for fear of tumbling head first into a rabbit hole of desire, passion, and an awkward morning after.

I have never been shy of one night stands, as my night with Ilana last month proved, but this is different. Worse yet, what if I make an assumption and it turns out I am wrong? How will I direct my prayers to him afterwards?

A line on the screen halts my spiralling thoughts, and I click the link. It's as I remembered, but I'm not certain whether that is good or bad for the investigation.

'Did you find something?' Wishearth asks.

'Jessika's ex-husband, Dharren Hardying, works in the family business. They're wholesalers in spell ingredients.'

Wishearth cocks his head. 'Meaning he had access to the ink that ruined Jessika's wedding dress.'

'Exactly.'

'Which makes him the obvious suspect.'

'Exactly again.'

'But you're not sure?'

'No,' I say. 'It took me less than five minutes to find that information. Anyone who knew Jessika during her first marriage would know what line of work Dharren was in. That makes him not just the obvious suspect but the obvious scapegoat.'

'Do you know who's behind these pranks?' Wishearth asks, serious.

'If I did, don't you think I would have put a stop to it already?'

'Only if you had proof. But what I'm curious to know is whether you already have an inkling and you're not so much investigating a case as trying to prove a theory.'

The question catches me by surprise. I sip my brandy while I consider how best to answer and I find my tumbler empty. Holding onto the laptop with one hand, I lean sideways to set the glass on the side table next to the sofa.

'I have an inkling, perhaps, but nothing more. The

feeling I have can't be called a theory yet, not when I haven't begun to unravel the why.'

'But you have the who and the how?'

'Maybe, maybe not. Too soon to tell.'

'You're not going to tell me, are you?' Wishearth asks, but there is no irritation on his face.

'Not yet, no.'

'Would you tell Karrion?'

Here is another question that needs careful consideration. Wishearth has always been mercurial in his moods, but he has never shown any sign that he considers Karrion competition, whether for my time or for my affection. Why should he, when the bond we share goes back years and is far beyond a friendship? But now I wonder if Wishearth is jealous of Karrion having a share in my working life. Wishearth may on occasion nudge me in the right direction with my investigations, but he has never asked to help or to solve crimes with me. Is that what he wants?

'No, I wouldn't tell Karrion,' I say before the silence goes on for too long. 'I might steer him along a certain path as part of dividing up the leads to follow, but I wouldn't necessarily share a hunch with him until it was a proper theory.'

'I see.'

The flames flare in Wishearth's eyes. He is pleased with my answer.

I return my attention to the computer and work in silence for some time. When I next look up, Wishearth is draining the last of the Guinness. He lifts his empty glass in my direction.

'Another round?'

'Go on then,' I say. 'It's not like I'm going anywhere.'

'Let's hope there are no more incidents tonight, otherwise you'll not be so much running to investigate as crawling along the corridors while trying not to sing or vomit.'

'I'll bet you'd enjoy watching that.'

'Perhaps I would, though it would hardly do your reputation much good. Still, if the worst comes to the worst, I promise to keep you upright, if not vomit-free.'

'How reassuring.'

'If you wanted emotional support, you should have summoned your apprentice rather than me.'

'If you're not here for emotional support, why did you come?' I ask, lips curling into a grin.

'Purely for entertainment.'

'You ought to have stayed in Old London.'

Wishearth pauses next to the fireplace, our empty glasses in hand. His head is tilted downwards, allowing his black hair to obscure his eyes so I miss some of his expression.

'I don't think so.'

He is gone before I have a chance to think of a response, leaving behind a wayward spark that hangs in the air for a few seconds before fading away.

I should focus on the computer, should continue to research the gossip about the old Mage families in Old London, but instead I end up staring at the flames. Only about half of what Wishearth says is serious. The trouble is, I have never been good at figuring out when he jests and when he wants me to believe him. Perhaps he doesn't know, or perhaps he finds it amusing to leave me wondering about the true meaning of his words.

Does the same apply to his touch? Does he flirt to

catch me off guard, or is there a deeper meaning behind his actions? This evening, he has treated me like an old lover rather than a friend, and I don't know how far to go in response.

My childhood at the Wild Folk conclave may have taught me the prayers and rituals to venerate the Hearth Spirits, but what they didn't provide was a roadmap for a friendship with a spirit.

'An offering for your thoughts?'

Wishearth has returned without my noticing, his feet materialising out of a plume of smoke even as I yank my eyes up.

'What?'

'You looked so lost in thought I wondered whether you needed a trail of breadcrumbs to find your way back. What were you thinking about with such intensity?'

'You.'

His expression registers fleeting surprise before he grins. 'Quite right. It's good to see you're on the right track at last.'

'I don't know. Perhaps I ought to watch myself in the future. Your ego doesn't need any more inflating.'

'Lady Bergamon said that to you, didn't she?'

It's my turn to look surprised, and he laughs.

'We've been friends for centuries,' he says and hands me another tumbler of brandy. 'I recognise her words even when they're spoken by someone else.'

He returns to his spot on the sofa and draws my feet across his lap again. While he was away, a nagging ache had wormed its way down my legs, but his heat banishes it. I lean my head back, enjoying a rare moment of being free from pain.

'Is it that bad?' Wishearth asks, his voice quiet.

I lift my head to look at him, but find only shadows on his face. 'Noticeable, rather than bad. In any case, I'm used to it.'

'You shouldn't have to be.'

'Life is rarely fair. We must live with the hand we've been dealt.'

The warmth against my legs intensifies, and it travels over my thighs and up my torso. I accept it with quiet gratitude, knowing he can offer temporary relief, but no cure.

I make a half-hearted attempt at continuing my research, but soon set the laptop aside. By the time I have finished the second brandy, the room is blurring around the edges. I was up early to walk Sinta and take her to the Open Hearth for the weekend, and the long day is beginning to weigh on me. Somewhere at the back of my mind I realise I forgot about dinner, but the thought is lost in a haze of alcohol.

Wishearth stays sprawled on the sofa as I retreat to the bathroom to brush my teeth and change into the T-shirt and yoga pants that serve as my pyjamas. He has not moved when I return and set up the spark guard in front of the fire, now burning low. I cross the room to the bed and slip under the covers, but do not lie down. Our eyes meet.

'Stay,' I whisper into the silence of the room.

He strides across the distance separating us and sits on the edge of the bed. I lie down, and Wishearth caresses my cheek with hot fingers.

'Sleep well, Yannia.'

# CHAPTER 7

I wake up to a feeling of suffocation. My adrenaline spikes, and I flail around, desperate for air. The ground disappears from beneath me, and I land on the floor with a thud. Something soft slides on top of me. My eyes fly open, but all I see is white.

Has the Winter Queen come to claim me? Has she yanked me from the dying lands to a world of snow and ice? Is this the end of me as I am, soon to be replaced by a bloodthirsty hound in the Fey pack?

The vision of white is replaced by Wishearth's face looming over me. He is holding onto something, which I recognise as a duvet. The carpet is scratchy against my cheek and my hip hurts where I landed on it.

'Is this how you get out of bed?' Wishearth asks. 'It would certainly explain why you sleep on a mattress on the floor.'

'What happened?'

I struggle onto my elbow and find myself next to the double bed. My mouth tastes like mothballs, and my temples are tightening with the first hint of a hangover.

'You fell out of bed.'

As much as I'd like to claim it's not true, I cannot

argue with the evidence before me. I rub my sore hip.

'It must have been one hell of a dream,' he says, and offers me a hand. His heat envelops me as he pulls me to my feet.

'It must have been, though I recall none of it.'

'Shame. By the way, you drool in your sleep.'

'I do not,' I say, and raise a hand to rub around my mouth.

Wishearth grins. 'Made you check.'

'Shut up.' I stagger to the bathroom.

A cool shower and brushing my teeth eases the hangover and helps clear my thoughts. Already I am cursing myself for not doing more work last night, but a part of me thinks I needed an evening of brandy, fire, and smoky company in ways that have little to do with the case.

When I step out of the bathroom, a towel wrapped around my torso, I find Wishearth straightening the pillows on the bed. As he turns to look at me, his gaze sets my exposed skin on fire.

'So you go beyond delivering drinks to maid service?' I ask, more to cover my embarrassment than because I feel like joking.

'For you, I'm willing to make an exception,' he says with a wink, but there are no flames in his eyes.

Unable to think of anything to say in response, I walk to my bag and pick out fresh clothes. If I only felt his eyes on me from the fireplace, I might drop the towel where I stand. But it is a step too far when he is standing mere yards away. I retreat to the bathroom.

'Are you coming down to breakfast?' I ask when I return, twisting my wet hair into a braid.

'I'm not mortal,' Wishearth says, and I think I detect

a hint of regret in his voice. 'I don't have the same needs as you do.'

It's an admission of more than not needing food, but how far it goes, I cannot tell. Here is yet another question I dare not ask for fear of causing offence. The list grows longer each time I'm with him.

'I can order breakfast from room service and stay here,' I say, when the silence begins to grow heavy.

'No need. You will want to check in with your assistant. There are plenty of fireplaces for me to investigate in this hotel. Who knows what secrets I might uncover along the way?'

'Are Jessika and Robbert safe?' I ask, cursing myself for taking so long to remember my request to Wishearth yesterday.

'Yes. They came in late, but both spent an uneventful night in their room.'

'That's something at least. I'll see you later.'

Wishearth steps closer, his fingers ghosting over my cheek, but never touching the skin. The heat radiating from him is a caress in itself, and I wonder if he can feel it like I can.

'When you need me, call, and I'll come.'

Before I have a chance to think of a reply, he fades into a cloud of smoke, leaving me alone in my room. I remain rooted to the spot for a moment longer, until my rumbling stomach sends me to the door.

The dining area is busy despite the early hour. Where yesterday stood a table large enough to accommodate all the wedding guests, many smaller ones are now dotted around. A breakfast buffet is laid out along one of the walls, and I head straight for the coffee pot.

It is rare for me to stay at a hotel, and I make full use of the buffet, especially the eggs section. Since I befriended Karrion, I have stopped buying eggs, making this a luxury. By the second cup of coffee and a fried breakfast, my hangover is a fading memory and I feel ready to tackle whatever the day will throw at me.

I have been the sole occupant of a table for almost an hour before Jessika and Robbert enter the dining room. They notice me, and Robbert wheels over while Jessika makes a beeline for the coffee. Perhaps she, too, is suffering after her late evening.

'Morning,' Robbert says, and nods to a waiter who comes to remove one of the chairs at the table.

'How was your spell-casting practice last night?'

'What if instead of answering, I told you that it's not wise to do shots before attempting long-distance spells?'

I grin. 'Go on, who's been turned into a hedgehog?'

'Thankfully, no one, but one of the groom's men was resembling a Smurf when I last saw him.'

'You turned him blue?' I ask, doing my best to stifle a giggle.

'Not me, of course, but the best man's aim wasn't quite what it should have been. And then there was the retaliation.'

'Please tell me you're having a rainbow-coloured best man?'

Robbert laughs. 'It would be appropriate, but alas, no. That said, his feet did briefly turn into blocks of stone.'

'Let me guess: the Smurf is an East Mage?'

'Yes, and prone to seeking revenge.'

'Now I'm worried about your wedding in a whole new way,' I say, imagining a series of escalating acts of revenge taking place while Jessika tries to walk down the aisle.

'Don't worry. The rest of the wedding party had a stern word with both of them. They're now under threat of curses ranging from overgrown toenails to non-existent libido if they so much as breathe in each other's direction during this weekend. They'll be on their best behaviour for the wedding.'

'I hope you're sure about that.'

'I am,' Robbert said, a smirk appearing on his lips. 'The best man and I have been friends for a long time. In my younger days, I was a keen photographer and my archives are extensive.'

'Social media is a wonderful place for reminiscing about the good old days.'

'Especially the days that involved certain parties only wearing a pink tutu and a slather of ketchup across his chest.'

'Do I want to ask?'

'I would not,' Robbert says, as Jessika arrives at the table.

'Morning,' I say as she takes a seat next to me. 'Are any of your bridesmaids pink or orange?'

'Robbert told you about last night, did he?' she asks, rolling her eyes as he wheels towards the buffet.

'He was bursting with glee. It had to be released somehow.'

Jessika shakes her head. 'I always thought an older partner meant someone with more maturity, but I've since discovered that the only difference is that they've had more time to do stupid things and then brag about them.'

'If you haven't accumulated a host of crazy stories,

have you truly lived?'

'Not you too?' she asks, looking both weary and curious.

I wink at her. 'That would be telling.'

She laughs and sips her coffee.

'Did you have a good time?' I ask.

'The club was great. We danced, had a few drinks, danced some more. It was a little loud, but the music was good. We left when the table next to ours put on an impromptu striptease show.'

'Men or women?' I ask, wondering whether I missed out on anything interesting.

Jessika seems to guess the direction of my thoughts. 'Both. And trust me, I would have gladly given them money to keep their clothes on.'

We both laugh.

'How was your evening?' she asks.

Robbert returns with a tray of food on his lap. He passes her a bowl of fruit salad. Calleigh sits next to Robbert, who slips a piece of bacon off his plate and feeds it to her.

'Quiet,' I say, taking a bite out of my croissant. Flakes of pasty and bits of apricot jam land on my plate.

'So there were no more incidents after we'd gone?' asks Robbert.

'None. Wishearth told me no one tried to sneak into your room during the night.'

'That's certainly a relief,' Jessika says. 'Please thank him for us.'

Robbert strokes her arm. 'I think we can do better than that. Perhaps after breakfast we'll rekindle the fire in our room and thank him ourselves.'

I smile. 'He'd like that.'

'But how does one speak to a Hearth Spirit?' Jessika asks.

'Well, last night I told him to shut up several times, while he accused me of parroting someone else's words. A typical evening for us.'

'How can you have such familiarity with a creature from another plane?'

'There was a time when I wondered that myself, but ultimately, I've known him my entire life. I didn't know it was Wishearth specifically I was speaking to, but he's always been there. When I moved to Old London and found him in my local pub, the relationship developed because he was a friend first and a Hearth Spirit second.'

Robbert and Jessika share a look I cannot decipher. When they return their attention to me, Jessika's eyes are wide with awe.

'I've never heard of a spirit befriending a mortal before,' she says.

'It does happen. Wishearth is friends with others in Old London. But as with many things about spirits, they tend to be secretive about their personal lives.'

Before either of them has a chance to reply, a dishevelled man with dark circles under his eyes hurries to our table and lays a hand on Robbert's shoulder. I recognise him as Robbert's best man, Jaike.

'Can I have a word, mate?'

'Would you please excuse me,' Robbert says, laying his napkin on the table and wheeling himself away from the table. Calleigh matches her steps to the speed of the wheelchair.

'What do you think that's about?' Jessika asks.

We both watch as Jaike leads Robbert to the door and

out into the entrance hall. Once there, he crouches down next to the wheelchair and begins speaking.

'I don't know.'

Measuring the distance between us and them, I consider using magic to sharpen my hearing. But there are too many conversations taking place in this room. They would overwhelm me. Besides, I have a feeling Jessika and I will find out soon enough what the man has to say.

My suspicion is confirmed when Robbert leans forward in his chair to look at us and beckons. Jessika and I rise without a word and hurry to him.

'Yannia, you remember Jaike,' Robbert says. 'Jaike knows that we've been investigating the sabotage attempts.'

'Has something else happened?' I ask, suspecting that we are about to receive more bad news.

'It's the rings,' Jaike says, a little breathless. The smell of old alcohol hangs heavy around him. 'I can't find them anywhere.'

# CHAPTER 8

'What?' Jessika says, loud enough that the word echoes around the hall. She lowers her voice. 'Sorry. But what do you mean, you can't find them anywhere?'

'They were on my nightstand when I left for your stag do yesterday evening. When I woke up this morning, they were gone.'

'What about when you arrived back last night?' I ask.

'I'm really sorry, but I was way too pissed to pay attention.'

'The rings can't be gone,' Jessika says, a note of hysteria creeping into her voice. 'How can they be gone? Who would have taken them?'

'I've spent the last hour turning my room upside down. I'm so sorry, both of you. I've screwed up.'

Jaike rubs his face with both hands. His stubble makes a scratching sound, and more of the old alcohol smell wafts from his body.

'Someone is trying to sabotage the wedding,' Robbert says. 'It's not your fault you're caught in the middle of it all.'

'I should have locked the rings in the safe or hidden them in a drawer, rather than leaving them in plain sight.'

'Robbert is right,' I say. 'Whoever took the rings would have done so regardless of any precautions you took. None of this is your fault.'

Beside us, Jessika is shaking. Calleigh whines, nudging her hand, which draws Robbert's attention away from Jaike. He pulls Jessika closer, until she is sitting on his lap. She buries her head in the crook of his neck.

'It will be okay, love.' He rubs soothing circles on her back. 'We'll find the rings. This, or anything else anyone throws us at will not stop us from having a magical day tomorrow. I promise.'

Under different circumstances, I might be tempted to warn Robbert against making such promises, when they are beyond his control, but I remain silent. Jessika needs reassurance, not cold logic. After a while, her shaking subsides, but her eyes are wide with shock when she looks up.

'Who could have done this?' she asks.

'We'll continue our investigation straight away,' I say, and Robbert nods. 'Would you like to finish your breakfast?'

'I couldn't possibly eat, not while my wedding day hangs in the balance.'

Something about her reaction strikes me as odd, but I cannot put my finger on what. It makes sense for her to be upset about the loss of the rings, and yet something is not right. I file the thought away for further consideration later, and offer her a reassuring smile.

'Do you want me to call someone? One of the bridesmaids? Or one of your friends? I'm not even going to suggest your mother.'

Jessika shudders. 'She's the last person I want to see right now. She'll find a way to tell me this is all my fault and if only I had been more refined and more aristocratic, none of it would have happened.'

Robbert hugs her closer. 'What can I do, my love? How can I make you feel better?'

'Just knowing you and Yannia are working on this is enough,' Jessika says with a watery smile. 'I think I'm going to go back to the room and lie down for a moment. There's still the matter of a ruined wedding dress too. It will be a busy day.'

'Take Calleigh with you. She'll give better cuddles than I can, plus she's not going to let anyone into the room, so you'll be perfectly safe.'

'Thanks.' Jessika kisses Robbert's cheek. 'I love you.'

'I love you too. Make sure you lift Calleigh onto the bed and off again.'

Jessika nods. Taking Calleigh's lead from Robbert, she heads for the lifts. Jaike is still rubbing his face, as if the motion will rid him of his hangover.

'What can I do to help?' he asks.

'What time did you leave your room for the stag do last night and when did you return?'

'We left here about six thirty and I got back to my room maybe half past one.' Jaike glances at Robbert, who nods. 'Five minutes later, I was asleep.'

'That gives our thief a generous window to break in and take the rings.'

'There's no guarantee that the theft didn't happen after we returned,' Robbert says. 'Anyone who saw the state of us would have known Jaike would have passed out as soon as he reached his bed.'

'Do you mind if we check your room?' I ask.

'Knock yourself out.' Jaike passes me his room key. 'I'll be in the dining room, drinking all the coffee and feeling shit about myself.'

He trudges off, shoulders slumped, and I feel a stab of sympathy for him. There are so many clichés about the best man forgetting to bring the rings to the wedding, and now he has lost both before the ceremony. I suspect it will be some time before he will drink again.

We take the lift upstairs in tense silence. Jaike's room is halfway down the corridor, between my room and the bridal suite. When I push open the door, the smell of sweat and old socks washes over us. I rub my nose.

The room is dark despite the late hour. I flick on the lights and walk to the window to open the curtains. As light floods in, a cool breeze tickles my cheek. I follow it to find the balcony door ajar.

'Look,' I say, pointing to the door.

'Another way in.' Robbert wheels closer.

I open the door. There is a step down to the balcony, which is large enough for a wrought iron table and two chairs. Given the late season, I cannot imagine anyone wanting to spend time outside. Then I catch a hint of a pungent smell and bend down to retrieve the end of a hand-rolled joint.

'This could explain why the door was open,' I say, showing the joint to Robbert, who remains in the doorway.

There are similar balconies on both sides of us. I walk to the railing to gauge the distance between them. A human would struggle to jump across, unless they were a gymnast or an athlete. Most spell casters would also hesitate before attempting the feat. But for a Wild Folk like myself, the distance is nothing. I imagine someone like a Cat Shaman would find the jump equally trivial.

The image of Fria floats across my mind again, but I dismiss it. Why would she be in a country hotel in Sussex?

'Do you know who occupies the rooms on either side?' I ask.

'No, but it should be easy enough to find out.'

'Tell me about the rings,' I say as I return inside. 'Were they expensive?'

'Mine is a plain platinum band, so not at all. Jessika's is a family heirloom. My grandmother passed the ring to me when I announced our engagement. She died two months later. The ring is white gold, with emeralds and sapphires. It's antique and insured for a great deal of money.'

To hide my smile, I turn to shut the balcony door. There is no arrogance in Robbert's voice, but his casual dismissal of the value of a platinum ring is reminder of the disparity in his wealth compared to mine. Hiring this hotel as the wedding venue alone must cost more than my annual rent.

'Do you know how many people knew Jaike had the rings?'

'I'm not sure, but as it's traditional for the best man to keep hold of the rings before the ceremony, anyone could have made an educated guess.'

We search the room, but aside from a wide selection of clothes scattered across the floor, nothing is out of place. Robbert pauses next to the empty fireplace.

'Do you think your Hearth Spirit friend saw something?' he asks.

'I'll ask him, but I doubt it. He won't have spent much time in the empty fireplaces of the hotel, not when I asked him to keep an eye on your room.'

'So this is another dead end?' Some of Robbert's enthusiasm for the investigation deflates.

'Not yet. We need to find out if anyone used a key card to enter while Jaike was out with you, and who is staying in the adjacent rooms. That may give us something else to pursue.'

'Yannia, be frank with me,' Robbert says, wheeling his chair to face me. 'Do you have any idea who's behind all this?'

'I had a theory,' I say, a little reluctant. 'But this morning's events make me think I was wrong.'

'Are you going to tell me?'

'Not right now. We need more information, and there's little more we can find out here.'

On our way to the reception desk, we stop by my room. It's in considerably less disarray than Jaike's, and Wishearth is lounging on the sofa. For once, no pint of Guinness is in sight.

'Miss me already?' he asks as we enter.

'We have a question for you. Did you happen to notice anyone stealing two wedding rings from the best man's room last night?'

In a typical Wishearth manner, he shrugs and makes himself more comfortable on the sofa. This is not the first time he has shown disregard for the concerns of mortals other than his friends.

'You asked me to keep an eye on the bridal suite. Between that and making sure you didn't fall off your bed, I had my flames full.'

'I did fall off my bed,' I say.

'And I was there to laugh at you.'

Aware that Robbert is watching us with a mixture of

curiosity and amusement, I resist the temptation to roll my eyes at Wishearth, who seems to enjoy my discomfort.

'I thought you probably hadn't seen anything, but I wanted to check just in case.'

'Had all the wedding guests lit a fire in their rooms and spoken a prayer to a Hearth Spirit, I could have extended my reach. As it was, I was limited to the fire-places with flames.'

'We understand,' Robbert says. 'And I'd like to thank you for your protection.'

Wishearth finally stands, smiling his best mysterious immortal spirit smile. The urge to roll my eyes behind Robbert's back grows stronger.

'You are welcome, mortal man. I hope you remember this when you depart for your own home and hearth. Loyalty rewards loyalty. It's been many a decade since anyone from your bloodline spoke words of thanks, though your servants kept up the habit long after you had forgotten the prayers and rituals of old.'

'I... I'm sorry,' Robbert says, taken aback by Wishearth's knowledge of his family. 'From now on, consider my household the most committed follower of the old ways.'

'Good.' Wishearth's eyes are engulfed by flames as he nods towards me. 'Yannia will remind you of the rituals.'

Understanding my part in this scene, I nod, trying my best to keep my expression solemn. 'As you wish, oh wisest of the Hearth Spirits.'

'You had to ruin it, didn't you?' Wishearth sighs.

'Who knows, perhaps one of these days you'll manage to convert all the aristocratic Mage families back to the old ways.'

'If only.'

Wishearth returns to the sofa, and Robbert and I take our leave. Once the door has closed behind us, he lays a hand on my arm.

'I'd very much like to learn the old rituals,' he says.

Nodding, I smile. 'Good. He may enjoy the occasional bout of mystery and melodrama, but Wishearth does reward loyalty. His warnings have helped me more than once.'

'Religion has never been a big part of my family's traditions, but now I wonder if we've forgotten something important.'

'You have,' I say. 'Though I would argue that honouring the Hearth Spirits has little to do with religion. What need have you for that, when you can conjure flames out of thin air? But since you know spirits are real and living among us, it is simply good sense to afford them the respect they deserve.'

'Wise words indeed,' Robbert murmurs as the lift doors ping open.

In the entrance hall, we head for the reception desk. An older woman I don't recognise is in the middle of a phone call, tapping away at the computer keyboard while she confirms the availability of rooms over Christmas. When the call ends, she smiles at us.

'Can I help you?'

I pass her Jaike's room key. 'Can you check your records for last night to see when a key card was used to access this room, please?'

She swipes the key card through a reader and passes it back to me, eyes focused on the monitor. 'It was used at five thirty yesterday evening and again at one thirty. After that, no one went in until about half an hour ago.'

'Thank you, we really appreciate your help. Could you also tell us who is occupying the rooms on either side of this one?'

'I'm afraid I can't tell you that. It's not policy to give out information about our guests.'

Robbert inches a little closer to the reception desk, raising his chin. In his posture and the imperious look he casts in the woman's direction, I can see the generations of Mages who flourished safe in the knowledge that they were better than all other magic users put together.

'Given that I have paid for every room in this hotel for the weekend, the least you can do is tell me which of my guests are occupying these particular ones.'

The woman hesitates and nods. She checks her computer. 'One of the rooms is occupied by Carrolyn Craichton and the other by Antonnio Bhartolli.'

'Thank you,' Robbert says and wheels himself away from the reception desk. I follow him until we are out of earshot.

'We need to speak to my sister.'

'I'm assuming you know who Antonnio Bhartolli is?' I ask.

'Yes. We met when I did a year abroad at Scuola di Magia in Rome and have been friends ever since.'

'Is he a Mage?'

'No. A Cat Shaman.'

Nothing further is needed to pique my interest. We check the dining room, but neither Carrolyn nor Antonnio are there. As we are heading towards the lifts, Carrolyn enters through the main doors. She is dressed in khaki trousers and a matching jacket, and her cheeks are red from the chill.

'Good morning, Robbert,' she says, affording me nothing more than a glance.

'Morning. We were heading upstairs to speak to you.'

'Both of you?' She includes me with the barest flick of an eyebrow.

'Yes,' says Robbert. 'There has been a development in the case.'

'I would hardly call a couple of dead doves a case.'

'You're forgetting what happened to Jessika's wedding dress,' Robbert says, and motions towards the lifts. 'Shall we? There are things we need to discuss with you and I'd prefer to do so in private.'

'Of course.'

We take the lift upstairs in an uncomfortable silence. Robbert sits between us, a tangible barrier against Carrolyn's dislike of me. This is not the first time a Mage has deemed me beneath them and not been afraid to show it, so I pay her no heed. In fact, I think she would learn a thing or two about disdain from Lord Ellensthorne, though I choose not to volunteer the introductions.

Carrolyn leads us to her room, which is to the left of Jaike's. It comes as no surprise that the room is immaculate. There is no sign that it's occupied at all. Once she has shut the door behind us, Carrolyn unzips her coat and hangs it in the wardrobe.

'What's so sensitive that it couldn't be discussed downstairs?' she asks, and takes a seat on one of the pale green sofas. Her posture is ramrod straight, her legs crossed at the ankles, and her hands resting on her lap, palms up.

'Someone broke into Jaike's room and stole the wedding rings last night.'

'Nana's ring is gone?'

'I'm afraid so.'

'But it's been in our family for generations.'

'I know.'

'Who could have taken it? Have you called the Paladins? Has the room been processed for traces of magic yet? How did the thief get in? Do you have any leads?'

'They likely went in through the balcony,' I say. 'All the entries using the room key tally with Jaike's movements, and the balcony door was ajar this morning.'

'Was the safe broken into? Surely someone must have heard something.'

'The rings weren't in a safe,' Robbert says.

'What?' Carrolyn's eyes flash with indignation. 'Our family heirloom stored somewhere other than a safe? I never heard anything so ridiculous. Does that man have no idea how valuable Nana's ring is?'

'No, I never told him. I didn't want him to be terrified.'

'And look where it led you. I simply cannot believe this.'

Carrolyn leaps up and paces across the room. Her fingers lace and unlace. Robbert wheels towards her and stops in her path. When she comes close enough, he takes her hands in his.

'We're going to find out who took the rings. It's going to be okay.'

'How can you possibly say that? You're hardly the finest detective in the Brotherhood of Justice.'

Robbert averts his face from her, as if stung by her words, and then returns to look at her. 'No, but I work with the best PI in Old London.'

'I'd hardly call her the best. Don't you remember

Jonathain Marsh?' Carrolyn drops her voice, but not enough to prevent me from hearing. 'How can you trust a savage like her to do anything other than eat raw meat with her bare hands and breed in primitive huts?'

'You are showing your privilege,' Robbert says, letting go of her hands. 'Mages aren't the only people of value, no matter what we've been taught to believe. You'd do well to think before speaking, especially in the presence of someone with enhanced senses.'

Carrolyn whips around to look at me. I meet her gaze without flinching or showing any sign of embarrassment at her assessment of me. While I may be of the Wild Folk, I can nevertheless match the coolness of an aristocratic Mage. The nobles of Old London aren't the only people capable of haughty aloofness. The Eldermen and, by extension, Dearon, would give even Lord Ellensthorne a run for his money.

'While I may be repeating known stereotypes about the Wild Folk, I'm not wrong about the Marsh case,' she says, unwilling to back down.

I say nothing. The truth is a secret I vowed to keep. Besides, I owe this woman no explanation.

'Carrolyn,' Robbert says, his tone frosty.

'Fine.' She lifts her hands in defeat and returns to her spot on the sofa. 'What do you want from me?'

'Did you spend the whole of yesterday evening at the hotel?' I ask.

'Yes. After lunch, I took a walk around the grounds for an hour and a half. The views are quite lovely, and there was no one about. I came up here and read until dinner. Rather than go downstairs, I ordered a salad from room service. I took a bath and went to bed around ten o'clock.'

'Did you hear anything from the room next door?' Robbert asks.

'Not that I recall. The walls are thick, and I don't make a habit of keeping my ears pricked for the neighbours' movements. I think I may have heard Jaike leave because I thought he was speaking to you in the corridor. You'd told me about your evening plans, so I chose not to go to the door and interrupt you.'

I perch on the edge of an armchair. 'What about after you'd gone to bed? Did anything disturb you during the night?'

'No, I slept soundly until the morning.'

'Was your balcony door open at any point?'

Carrolyn snorts. 'It's the end of November. We civilised people prefer to stay warm and comfortable in our houses, rather than roaming through the rain and muck of the countryside.'

'Carrolyn,' Robbert says, and this time his tone is so cold I can hear the chime of icicles.

'It's true. The Wild Folk live in dens rather than houses. I doubt they feel the cold at all.'

'We feel the cold,' I say, my voice steely. 'And we have houses. Probably not proper by your standards, but they have doors and windows and beds.'

'How marvellous,' Carrolyn says, her lips pressing into a thin smile. 'Even the animals are crawling towards the twenty-first century.'

'That's enough.' Robbert's words are accompanied by a surge of power, which sets my teeth on edge. 'I have had quite enough of your insults, both those aimed at Yannia and Jessika. You'd do well to remember that I am free to choose my friends and loved ones.'

'You are free, yes, but that doesn't mean you have the necessary skills to do so.'

'I think we've asked all the questions we need to for now,' I say, standing up. 'Robbert, we have a lot to do. Shall we?'

Robbert and Carrolyn stare at each other. A faint scent of dust and sun-baked salt swirls in the air, stirred by the rising power of two South Mages. Robbert is the first to look away, nodding at me.

'You're right. Let's go.'

'Thank you for your time,' I say to Carrolyn.

She only stares at me, her face puckered as if she has eaten something sour. I follow Robbert to the door and close it behind us.

# CHAPTER 9

Out in the corridor, Robbert's stiff posture relaxes and he rubs a hand over his face. I lead him away from Carrolyn's door in case she is listening.

'I'm sorry,' Robbert says. 'She's not usually as venomous as that. I'm not sure what's got into her recently.'

'What was that about her not liking Jessika?' I ask.

'That's another mystery. When I first introduced them a year ago, Carrolyn was cautious, but polite. At one point, I thought they might even become friends, though Jessika is much younger. But a couple of months ago, Carrolyn suddenly became cold towards her.'

'Does she object to the wedding?'

'I'm not sure she's thrilled about it...' Robbert trails off and snaps his head up to look at me. 'You can't possibly think that Carrolyn is behind these attempts to sabotage our wedding?'

'It's a possibility. Given the account she gave of her movements yesterday, she doesn't have much of an alibi. It would have been easy for her to break into Jaike's room at any point in the evening, while the members of the stag party were away from the hotel. As for the other two incidents, all she would have needed was money to bribe a member of staff.'

'I can't imagine her leaping from balcony to balcony to steal the rings. She seemed genuinely upset about the theft.'

'You're right, it's unlikely she did it herself. But there are plenty of other options.'

Perhaps I ought to check that Fria is in Old London, though she will have had enough time to return to the city after breaking into Jaike's room last night. But hiring a thief like Fria suggests premeditation that goes beyond even obtaining a bottle of magical ink. I will have a word with her, just in case. Even if she had nothing to do with the theft, she may have heard something among her shadier contacts.

'You think Carrolyn hired someone,' Robbert says.

'I'm not sure what to think. Let's speak to Antonnio. He may have heard or seen something.'

We knock on Antonnio's door. While we wait, I borrow the hearing of a mouse scurrying within the walls. Faint footsteps move around inside the room, before approaching the door. It opens.

A man dressed in a deep red dress shirt and black slacks stands in the doorway. His dark hair is greying at the temples, and he has a closely cropped salt-and-pepper beard. Cautious eyes sweep over us, but a degree of warmth softens them when he spots Robbert.

'Morning, Robbert,' he says, with a thick Italian accent.

'Buongiorno, Antonnio,' Robbert replies, and is rewarded with a smile. 'Do you mind if we come in? There are some questions we'd like to ask you.'

Antonnio's expression flickers to curiosity and then indifference. He shrugs and steps aside.

Apart from the colour of the wallpaper and the soft

furnishings, the room is identical to Jaike's and Carrolyn's. Antonnio settles in one of the armchairs with the grace of a cat, one leg dangling over the armrest. He looks like a great hunter at rest, his relaxed pose hiding the power he possesses.

'Were you here yesterday evening?' Robbert asks.

'Yes, it is very quiet after the noise of Rome. Good for yoga on the balcony.'

'Isn't it a bit cold?' I ask.

Antonnio quirks one perfectly shaped eyebrow at me. 'Cold is nothing to a cat.'

'What time were you doing your yoga?' asks Robbert, leaning forward in his wheelchair.

'Between seven and nine. I like the slow, mindful practice.'

'Did you see or hear anything strange, especially coming from the room to your left?'

'What is strange? People do all kinds of strange things in hotels and in their homes.'

'What Robbert means is did you see anyone gain entry to the hotel room via the balcony?'

Antonnio's lips curl into a slow grin. 'They would have needed skill to make the leap. A human couldn't do it. A Mage, perhaps. But once they were on the balcony, the rest, it is easy.'

'Why?' I ask, though am I beginning to feel like Antonnio is toying with us as a cat might play with a mouse.

'The balcony door was ajar. Had been all evening.'

'How do you know?' Robbert asks.

'I notice things. It is important in my profession.'

'What do you do?'

'I'm a journalist. The newspaper catering to the magical district of Rome wants me to write an article about the wedding. Even in Italia, we like to hear the news about the European Mage aristocracy. It is shaping up to be quite the weekend. My editor, she will be pleased.'

'How do you mean?' I ask, feigning innocence.

'The doves in the dining room, a ruined wedding dress, and now the rings have gone missing. It sounds like someone is not so happy about the match.'

'How do you know all that?' Robbert asks, eyes wide with astonishment.

'He's a Cat Shaman,' I say with a small sigh. 'His ears are as sharp as a leopard's, and he has a nose for a story.'

Antonnio smiles, revealing canines that are long and sharp. Were he not sitting in direct sunlight, I might reconsider my stance of vampires being a myth.

'You are right, Wild Woman. You can find out much if you know when to listen.'

'Do you know who's behind it all?' Robbert asks.

Staring at us with obvious pleasure, Antonnio takes his time stretching. Despite his position draped across the chair, he manages to look immaculate and alluring. There is shrewdness in his eyes, as if he was hoping one of us would ask the question.

'No.'

As soon as he speaks, I am certain he is lying. Our eyes meet, and his chin lifts in a subtle challenge. I want to call him out, but all I have is an instinct. To get the better of him, I will need irrefutable proof.

'So you didn't see anyone going into Jaike's room last night?' Robbert says, and I wonder whether he missed the brief exchange between me and Antonnio.

'The Mage was out until the early hours of the morning. I saw no one enter or exit his room through the balcony.'

The way he speaks gives deliberate meaning to each word, and I am left trying to discern his true message. For now, it eludes me.

'All right, thanks for speaking to us,' Robbert says. 'Will you sit with me and Jessika at lunch? She's been wanting to find out all the secrets from our university days and I'd rather she interrogates you than me.'

Antonnio laughs. 'With pleasure.'

We are heading for the door, when I notice something on the floor between the bed and a nightstand. It looks like a piece of green silk, a scarf perhaps. When I look up, Antonnio is watching me, and I am struck with the thought that he wanted me to see it. But why?

As soon as the door closes behind us, Robbert turns to me, a question on his lips. I shake my head, Antonnio's words about knowing when to listen echoing in my mind. He seems to understand my reluctance, and we head for the lifts in silence.

Once we reach the ground floor, I direct us out through the main doors, down the ramp next to the steps, and around the building. There are paved paths around the immediate grounds, and we choose one that leads directly away from the hotel. I keep an eye on the distance, measuring how far a cat's hearing might extend, and after I am satisfied that we are out of range, I keep going for another minute. Caution is a virtue I have learnt over the course of my career as a PI.

A chill wind tugs at our clothes as we approach the shore of a small lake. I glance at Robbert, concerned that we should have picked up coats from our rooms. It would be bad form for me to cause the groom to catch a cold a day before his wedding. As if sensing my thoughts, Robbert leans to the side and picks up a long stick. He wheels around me in a small circle, dragging the stick along the ground, until he has marked an area with both of us within it. My innate sense of magic feels his aura stretching outwards, seeking power. I have often wondered how a Mage casts spells and how they view the power within the world, but I have never had an opportunity to ask. It's something I ought to raise with Tinker Thaylor when I next speak to her.

Robbert utters words of power, and a warm southerly wind caresses my cheek. It fills the area around us with the heat of the noonday sun, the warmth of the afternoon, the velvet softness of nights in the south. The heat is oppressive, giving me an urge to break the boundary and flee, but I swallow back the discomfort. Robbert cast the spell with my wellbeing in mind, and it would be rude to refuse the kindness.

'Are we far enough away that we won't be overheard?' he asks.

'I think so.'

Just in case, I draw upon the web of all living things and sharpen my hearing until the clink of silverware being arranged in the hotel's dining room becomes as clear as if the table was next to us. Although it is distracting, nothing can approach us without my knowing it.

'So, what do you think?' Robbert asks.

'About Antonnio? He knows more than he lets on.'

'I had the same impression. But if he knows who is sabotaging my wedding, why won't he tell me?'

'Because by choosing to stay silent, he is gaining something more valuable to him than your gratitude.'

'That seems cynical.'

'I've spent enough time in the company of a Cat Shaman to have an inkling of how they think. Never forget they are cats first and foremost. It's not beyond the realms of possibility that they would cause chaos simply for the sake of chaos, though I don't believe that to be the case with Antonnio. Something else is going on.'

'How do we find out what?'

'It could be that we too need to figure out when to speak and when to listen.'

'Are you suggesting we start eavesdropping?' Robbert asks, his tone affronted.

'No, not at all. But I'm starting to think that there is more going on than I had initially appreciated. Our challenge is to separate the facts from the background noise.'

'How do we do that?'

'For one, I will need to have a word with my apprentice. He may have found something in the research he's conducting that will help us. I would also suggest that as much as you'd like Antonnio to entertain Jessika over lunch, we both keep a close eye on your guests. If anyone is acting strangely or seems to be interacting with people they normally wouldn't be talking to, we need to know about it.'

Robbert glances at his watch. 'Not to rush the investigation, but I'm supposed to be getting married in twenty-four hours, and at present my bride doesn't have a dress and neither of us have wedding rings.'

'Jessika is resourceful. She will no doubt find another

dress in time. As for the rings, once we track down the person sabotaging your wedding, we'll recover the rings.'

'Assuming they haven't already been taken away from the hotel and pawned.'

'I don't think so,' I say, my words slow. 'There were other things someone could have stolen in Jaike's room. If this was a general theft rather than a targeted attack, we would have heard of jewellery and other valuables going missing from the other rooms as well. Whoever took the rings was after them specifically, I'm sure of it.'

'What do we do now?' Robbert asks.

'Why don't you check in with Jessika? She will want reassurance that we are working as hard as we can. I'll speak to my apprentice. Shall we meet at the bar in half an hour?'

'All right.'

Robbert propels his chair forward, breaking the spell's barrier. Straight away, a gust of cold wind steals away the warmth, and a tightness around my torso lifts. I can breathe freely again. When I don't move to return to the hotel with Robbert, he pauses.

'Will you be all right out here? It's pretty cold.'

'I'm resistant. The cold doesn't bother me much.'

In his eyes, I see a desire to ask questions, but his manners prevent him from prying. He nods and leaves me without another word.

As I turn towards the lake, I wrap my arms around my torso. I do feel the cold, not as a chill wind freezing me to my core, but as a whisper of a homeland I have never been to. The Winter Queen would welcome me at her halls. All I would have to do is kneel before her and accept my fate as one of her faithful hounds. But, that I will not do, not now, not ever. Whatever the price for remaining me, I must one day pay it.

Before my thoughts turn too dark, I fish around in my pocket for my phone. A distant part of me tracks the crunch of gravel beneath the tyres of Robbert's wheelchair as he approaches the hotel. I need not face that way to know if anyone tries to sneak up on me. For the time being, the wind and the grey skies mean that I have the lake to myself.

Karrion doesn't answer my call. I leave him a voice-mail asking him to call me back when he is free. Try as I might, I cannot remember him saying anything about plans for the weekend. Not that it matters, for he has the weekend off and he is free to spend it as he pleases.

With nothing further keeping me by the water, I meander back towards the hotel, taking my time. I use the walk as an opportunity to review the case so far, but my thoughts keep coming back to Antonnio. Something he said is bothering me, but every time I think I am closing in on the answer, it slips between my fingers.

My prolonged period outside means that by the time I reach the main doors, I'm shivering and my nails are blue. I slip inside, and the wall of warmth washing over me brings welcome relief. Blowing on my fingers, I rub my hands together as I wait for the numbness to recede.

I am still standing there, flexing my fingers and wondering whether to go upstairs to my room to seek out Wishearth and his warmth, when Jessika calls my name from the lifts.

'There you are, Yannia,' she said, hurrying towards me. Robbert and Calleigh follow behind her. 'Lunch is served.'

'Thanks.'

Jessika leads the way to the dining room, where the table settings are mercifully devoid of dead doves. She indicates that I should sit next to her. Antonnio approaches us and takes the seat on her other side, with Robbert to his right. Calleigh settles behind Robbert and lays her head on her paws. There is no grey in her muzzle, but she acts like a dog weighed down by years. I find this odd, when she has spent the morning curled up in bed with Jessika, rather than following Robbert and I around the hotel.

'How goes the hunt for a new wedding dress?' I ask while a waiter pours white wine into our glasses.

'I have something special figured out. But tell me, have you any more thoughts on who could have taken the rings? I can't bear the thought that someone has stolen them and sold them in a dingy pawn shop somewhere. The ring I was to have is part of Robbert's family history.'

'No thoughts yet, though we have many leads to pursue,' I say, aware of Antonnio sitting close by.

'I do hope so. This whole weekend has been terrible for my nerves. I'm not sure even three weeks in the Maldives will cure me of my constant fear of something else bad happening.'

'You'll feel better once the culprit, or culprits, have been apprehended.'

'Do you think there is more than one person involved?' Jessika looks around the tables at the guests streaming in.

'Without a doubt. The better question is how many people are involved.'

'How many?' Jessika asks, her voice reedy.

'I'll figure it out. It's your wedding gift, after all.'

Jessika smiles, but it comes out as little more than a twitch of her lips. A waiter sets bowls of soup before us, and she drops her attention to her plate.

Antonnio pushes his chair back with a squeak and bends to peer under the table. Jessika pauses while laying a napkin on her lap and turns to him.

'Is everything all right?'

'I think I dropped my phone.'

With Antonnio disappearing under the table, Jessika sets her napkin aside and rises. She pulls her chair back and Robbert reverses, disturbing Calleigh's rest. I also stand and crouch to look under the table. Footsteps approach and stop behind us.

'Are you feeling ill, Robbert?' Carrolyn's voice sounds from above me.

'I'm fine. Antonnio dropped his phone.'

'Oh. So you're fine?'

'Yes, I'm perfectly fine,' says Robbert with a hint of exasperation.

I shift out from under the table, narrowly missing catching my temple against the edge. Carrolyn is standing with a hand on Robbert's shoulder, her purse clutched under one arm. Around us, waiters are delivering soup bowls to further guests. Calleigh whines, and Robbert pets her head.

'I found it.' Antonnio emerges, waving his phone. 'These trousers have such small pockets. I shan't be careless like this again. Thank you, everyone, and apologies for delaying the start of your meal.'

We all move to return to our lunch, but Carrolyn

remains standing. I'm left with the impression that she is waiting for something; an invitation to join us, perhaps? Whatever she wants, it appears not to be forthcoming, and she sighs.

'If you are sure, Robbert. I'd hate to see you fall ill on the eve of your wedding. You shouldn't go outside without a coat, not in late November.'

'I'm a South Mage, as you well know,' Robbert says, and the strained patience in his voice is obvious to all present. 'Keeping warm has never been an issue.'

'Of course. You know best, as you always do.'

Carrolyn hurries away, and Robbert stares after her with a look that is half-exasperation, half-regret. But he doesn't say anything and instead instructs Calleigh to lie down again. We sit down, and he moves closer to the table.

The soup is bright orange. It has a smoky aftertaste that is almost bitter. I prefer my food simpler than this. I struggle to identify the many spices and ingredients, but I eat it without comment. Jessika asks Antonnio about his time in university with Robbert, and I am content to listen to the conversation. As soon as we have finished the soup, waiters replace our bowls with the main course: a rack of lamb with winter vegetables.

I am halfway through when a shiver runs down my spine. Glancing over my shoulder towards the fireplace, I note the fire is still burning. A bead of sweat slides down my temple just as my stomach cramps. I set my knife and fork down. A ball of nausea twists in my belly, sending a wave of pain down my legs. When I reach for my water glass, my hand is trembling.

'Are you okay?' Jessika asks. Her voice sounds strained.

'Yes. No. I don't feel well. I think I'm going to lie down for a bit.'

Standing up only makes the pain worse. I hurry towards the door. Among the hum of many conversations, I catch a concerned note when Robbert speaks. I look back and see Jessika standing, her face flushed. She is clutching her stomach and her eyes are tight with pain. Then a vicious cramp refocuses my attention on reaching my room. I take the stairs two at a time, clutching the banister for support, and half-run down the corridor. When I try to insert the key card into the lock, my hands shake so much it takes me three attempts to open the door.

Wishearth is lounging on the sofa. I stumble inside, trying to maintain my balance in the swaying room, and the key card falls from my fingers. He glances up, and the smile that was forming turns into a frown.

'Yannia? What's wrong?'

I try to tell him I feel sick, but another wave of nausea propels me towards the bathroom. With a hand clapped over my mouth, I make it just in time. The tiled floor is cold under my knees while I throw up everything I have eaten since waking up. Long after my stomach has emptied, the dry heaves keep me stuck to the spot. When at last they begin to subside, I pull myself up and rinse my face and mouth with cold water. I look at my reflection in the mirror. My eyes are rimmed with red and my cheeks are flushed. I touch my lips, and they tingle. All strength seems to have left my body, and it takes all my willpower to stumble out of the bathroom and to my bed.

While I was throwing up, Wishearth has closed the door to the corridor. He comes to me now, taking my elbow and guiding me to sit on the edge of the bed. I go to kick off my shoes, but he removes them for me. There is strange intimacy in the act, but there are no flames in his eyes as he watches me, only concern. He pulls the jumper over my head and guides me to lie down.

The sheets feel ice-cold against my bare skin, and I shiver. Wishearth pulls the covers up and then leans over me. I want to protest that I was just sick, but he inhales deeper than any mortal could. His face twists in anger.

'Stay there and don't move. I'll be back as soon as I can.'

He strides to the fireplace and vanishes before I have a chance to ask where he thinks I would go. But as my teeth chatter, I wish he hadn't gone at all. If he had stayed, he could have lain down next to me and warmed me. A tear slides down my cheek, over my ear, and into the pillow. Why didn't he understand I needed him to stay? Why would he leave me now?

Shudders wrack my body, forcing me to shut my eyes and clench my teeth. The nausea roils in my stomach, turning into a ball of fire that sets my insides aflame. I would double over in pain, but the tingling has spread from my lips to my arms and legs. They are paralysed, and the realisation turns my pulse erratic. A heavy weight spreads over my chest, making each breath a struggle. Is this how it will end, with my fighting for air, conscious until death claims me?

It occurs to me for the first time that perhaps I am not sick, but before the thought goes any further, I slip into blessed darkness.

# CHAPTER 10

I wake up to find that Wishearth has returned. He is lifting my head as he presses a cup to my lips. A trickle of liquid runs down the side of my mouth and soaks into the collar of my T-shirt. The weight on my chest has grown, and my brain is foggy from the lack of air.

'Drink,' he whispers.

I open my lips and some of the cool liquid slides down my throat. It tastes sweet and bitter, and like... coffee. I try to pull back, but Wishearth keeps the cup pressed against my mouth.

'You need to drink all of it, no matter how bad it tastes.'

As objections are impossible, I do as he says. There is a smoky residue at the bottom of the cup and it reminds me of charcoal. Why would Wishearth give me charcoal and coffee?

When the cup is empty, he lays my head on the pillow. He remains looming over me, eyes sharp as he searches for something on my face. The liquid sits uneasily in my stomach, the nausea rearing again now I have ingested something new. What if I have to vomit again? I cannot move and the thought of being sick on myself in front of Wishearth fills me with shame so strong that tears rise to my eyes.

'How do you feel?'

I don't know how to answer, or even if I can. My throat aches, as if filled with a hundred tiny cuts, and I long for the cooling touch of the Winter Queen. In this moment, I would gladly yield to her claim if she could only put out the flames burning me alive.

'What...?' It takes three tries to get the word out.

'You were poisoned with wolfsbane. When this is all over and done, I will laugh at how ironic that is, but for now, I'm looking to set someone on fire.'

There are flames in Wishearth's eyes, but they are not the slow, sensual kind I sometimes catch glimpses of when we are alone. Instead, a white inferno rages within him, and I fear for the person who did this.

My thoughts remain sluggish, but there is something important I know I have forgotten. Something that could be the difference between life and death. I think back to the lunch and recall Jessika's flushed face as she rose from the table.

'Jessika,' I croak. 'I think she was poisoned too.'

Wishearth rises in a motion too fluid for a mortal and picks up the cup he has placed on the nightstand.

'We don't have a moment to waste. I'll be right back.'

He strides to the fire before I have a chance to object and disappears again. I need to get up and go to Jessika. There's no telling whether she made it as far as her hotel room. What if she collapsed in the lift or in the corridor outside her room? I need to help her or at least call for help. But my limbs will not move and I remain paralysed in the bed. My concern for Jessika winds tighter and tighter into panic until my shallow breathing sends me back into the darkness.

*

When I open my eyes, the room has grown dark. The last rays of dusk are fading outside, and the only source of light in the room comes from the small fire still burning. Wishearth has kept it going all day.

I shift, testing the extent of the paralysis. My hand twitches, but it's as though my bones have been filled with lead. As I lie there, willing my muscles to work, I become aware of how hot I am under the covers. When I tilt my head to the side, I find Wishearth lying next to me. He is on his side, facing me, but in the gloom of the evening, his expression is impossible to read.

'Jessika?' I ask, after clearing my throat.

'She's asleep.'

Before I have time to consider the implications of lying in bed with Wishearth, he rolls away from me and off the bed. I swallow my disappointment and watch him circle to my other side. He tilts my head up, picks a cup from the nightstand, and brings it to my lips.

'Drink.'

The medicine, for that is what it must be, tastes no better the second time round, but the faint movement in my hand means that it's working. After I have drunk the lukewarm liquid, Wishearth changes the cup for a glass of water. I gulp it down, grateful to chase away some of the strange taste from my mouth. A few droplets of water spills from the corner of my lips, and Wishearth wipes them away with hot fingers.

As he rests my head back on the pillow, a memory half-buried rises to the surface. I remember where I last caught one of the scents in the medicine.

'Is there belladonna in that?' I ask, grateful that my voice is returning.

'Yes. One poison is an antidote for another.'

'But what about belladonna poisoning?'

'Lady Bergamon said that in these quantities, the coffee in the mixture counteracts any of the belladonna symptoms.'

'You went to Lady Bergamon for help?' I ask, and immediately feel foolish for stating the obvious.

'Yes.'

'How did you know what I'd been given?'

'There was a shadow of it stretched over your aura when you walked in. Didn't you see it in the bathroom mirror?'

'I can't see auras. No mortal can.'

'Oh. Of course. To me it was obvious. All I had to do was describe the effect on your aura and the scent of it to Lady Bergamon. She knew straight away what it was and your symptoms confirmed it. Fortunately, making a cure was straightforward.'

'Lucky indeed. I will have to thank her when I return to Old London.' Sleep weighs heavily on me, but I refuse to yield to it just yet. 'And Jessika? Is she okay?'

'After I burst out of the fireplace in a cloud of smoke, both her and Robbert were more likely to die from a heart attack. She was very ill, but I administered the cure in time before the poison did any permanent damage. What's curious is that her symptoms were less severe than yours.'

'Perhaps she ingested less of the poison,' I say, trying to marshal my thoughts. They remain sticky and scattered.

'It could be.' Wishearth lifts the cover and takes my hand in his. 'Yannia, there was a moment I thought I was going to lose you.'

I stare at him, but there are no sparks flying from his eyes. He is serious.

'Was it that bad?'

'When I returned with the first cup of the antidote, you were barely breathing. Had I been a few minutes later, who knows if you'd still have been alive.' He rests his forehead against the back of my hand. 'I'm sorry.'

'Hey, stop that,' I say. More than anything, I wish I could reach out and hug him, but my body refuses to move. 'You saved my life. Instead of apologising, you need to start telling me how I can't manage without you so that I can laugh and agree.'

He looks up, eyes black. Heat spreads from his fingers through my arm and it melts away some of the paralysis. With an effort that causes sweat to bead on my forehead, I lift my hand, and cup his cheek. He closes his eyes and leans into the touch, but says nothing.

'Thank you, Wishearth. I don't know how I'd manage without you.'

When he speaks, he keeps his eyes closed and the words are so soft I struggle to make them out.

'I've known you for so long I had forgotten how fleeting mortal lives are. You reminded me of a loss I wasn't yet ready to face. I doubt I'll ever be ready to face it.'

'One day you must,' I say, matching his soft tone. 'But not today.'

With what little strength I have, I draw him closer. He seems to understand, for he lifts the covers further and stretches out next to me. His warmth envelops my body, and it eases the paralysis. Wishearth slips an arm under my neck and shifts to his side, facing me. Under the scrutiny of his dark eyes, I am aware of the clammy T-shirt sticking to my skin and the fact that my breath must smell of belladonna and charcoal. But there is a steadiness to his gaze that sees beyond my flaws, and I am silently grateful for him.

A buzzing in my back pocket yanks me from my contemplation of Wishearth. I try to reach for the phone, but my tingling hands refuse to work. Wishearth realises what I am trying to do and slides a hand under me to retrieve the phone. He glances at the screen.

'It's Karrion,' he says, and declines the call.

'But I wanted to talk to him.'

'Not tonight. You need to rest.'

'You do realise he's going to call again.'

Wishearth turns my phone in his hands a few times, before finding the power button. He switches off the phone and sets it on the nightstand, well out of my reach.

'Now he won't,' Wishearth says with a hint of smugness in his voice.

'It may have been important.'

'More important than recovering from wolfsbane poisoning?'

His words prompt a distant memory of something Wishearth said. I sift through fragments of fear, pain, and panic, until I remember his exact words.

'You said earlier that you thought a wolfsbane poisoning was ironic. Why?'

He raises an eyebrow. 'You don't think a Wild Folk being given wolfsbane is ironic?'

'I suppose. But what about Jessika? She's a South Mage.'

'She received a much smaller dose. I believe you were the intended target.'

'Why poison me?'

'You veered too close to the truth. Why else?'

'Yes, but so far everything that has gone wrong has been a little more than a prank. The doves may have looked gruesome, but the way they were killed and the reason for it was humane. Why would anyone suddenly graduate to attempted murder? It's a serious jump.'

'Could there be more at stake now?'

'I don't see how,' I say, blinking to keep my eyes from closing. As much as I want to fall asleep, solving this case is more important. 'Like I said, they're just pranks. Who'd be prepared to poison someone to avoid being caught for ruining a wedding dress?'

'What if there's more going on than you realise?'

'Like what?' I ask, the cold fear of failure gripping my insides. 'What have I missed?'

Wishearth sends a soothing wave of warmth over me. 'I don't know. It was just a thought. I think the husband is behind this.'

'The ex-husband or the husband-to-be?'

'Robbert. If it's not the butler, then it's always the spouse. Isn't it?'

'Not always. In this instance, I don't think it is Robbert. He's been nothing but helpful since we joined forces.'

'Couldn't it be false helpfulness?'

'No,' I say. 'He's been far more persuasive with the hotel staff than I could have managed on my own. Besides, what possible reason would he have to stop the wedding when he's the one paying for it all?'

'Why do mortals ever commit crimes?' Wishearth shrugs as best he can while lying down. 'Passion, money, revenge. Take your pick. Perhaps he's found someone else and doesn't want to marry Jessika. It's cheaper to sabotage the wedding to a point where she's too frightened by the pranks to proceed with the ceremony than to pay for a divorce a few months down the line.'

'That's so cynical.' I try to laugh, but all I can manage is a strangled croak. 'Besides, Robbert and Jessika love each other. It's one of the few things I'm certain of when it comes to this mystery. He would never hurt her, even if he was prepared to poison me.'

'But what if she was never meant to receive any of the wolfsbane?'

'He wouldn't be so careless as to accidentally poison his bride.'

Another thought tugs on the edge of my mind, demanding attention. Before I can focus on it, I yawn wide enough that my jaw cracks. Wishearth's eyes cloud with concern.

'You should rest,' he says.

'I have a case to solve and it became a whole lot more serious this afternoon.'

'You'll see things clearer in the morning. Sleep now, sleuth later.'

'No, we should check up on Jessika to make sure she's—'

Wishearth stops me by pressing a finger against my lips. My eyes widen.

'Yannia,' he says, his tone carrying a warning.

'But,' I try to object, all too aware how my lips brush against his finger pad.

'Sleep.'

He removes his finger, and I offer no further objection.

We are so close I could count his eyelashes. The embers of an old fire smoulder in his pupils, and once again I am reminded of how beautiful his flames are. It would be so easy to shift closer, to bring our bodies flush together. But my limbs refuse to move. Perhaps it is for the best. I am teetering on the edge of an unknown, and one more step will send me stumbling down a path from which there is no returning.

'Sleep,' Wishearth says again, and he leans closer to press a kiss on my forehead.

I close my eyes, focusing on my tripping heart. Whether its erratic thump is because of the poison and the antidote, or because of Wishearth's proximity, I cannot tell. The conundrum distracts me enough that the fatigue gains an upper hand, and I drift peacefully into sleep.

# CHAPTER 11

The bed shifts. Years spent sleeping alone have left me alert enough that the movement drags me awake. I open my eyes to find Wishearth standing beside the bed facing away from me, stretching his back. He must sense my gaze, for he turns and smiles.

'Good morning. How are you feeling?'

It is only then that I realise light is streaming in through the windows. Wishearth must have forgotten to draw the curtains last night, or more likely, it never occurred to him to do so. With a jolt, I realise that Jessika and Robbert will be getting married in a few short hours, assuming no one manages to stop the wedding.

I pull back the covers and in doing so, notice that my arms and legs are moving properly. The air is cool against my skin, and I shiver. My T-shirt is sticky with sweat; a side effect from sharing a bed with a Hearth Spirit. A nagging ache settles in my hips. Last night was the only respite from the pain I am likely to get.

'Better, I think,' I say when the silence has gone on for too long. 'Though I'm in desperate need of a shower.'

Shifting aside the rest of the covers and swinging my legs over the edge of the bed, I rise. As soon as I am upright, my legs buckle and I pitch forward. Wishearth catches me before I fall, and I end up with my face buried in his jumper, grateful that he cannot see my embarrassed grimace. His clothes smell of smoke, of course, and the scent soothes my racing thoughts as he helps me back to a standing position. My legs are weak, but with his arm around me, I manage to shuffle forward. As we inch our way across the room, it strikes me as odd that he is taking so much of my weight, when on the night of Samhain he refused to help me carry Lady Bergamon. Why is this time different? I want to ask the question, but when he turns to look at me, there is such intensity in his eyes that I lose the thread of my thoughts.

'Do you need help undressing?' he asks when we reach the bathtub and he lowers me to sit on the edge.

There is no hint of flirtation or amusement in his voice, and for that, I am grateful. He drapes a fresh towel over the rail above the bath.

'I should be okay, thanks.'

'Give me a moment, and I'll bring you fresh clothes.'

He leaves before I have a chance to reply and soon returns with jeans, T-shirt, and underwear, which he sets down on the counter. His silence unnerves me. The Wishearth I am used to would make a joke about my pink bra or the corgi socks. But the Hearth Spirit before me only turns to stare at me with a frown.

'Will you manage?'

'I'll sit on the edge of the tub while I shower. The floor is tiled, so it doesn't matter if it gets wet.'

'Good. If you need me, I'll be right outside. Shout, and I'll come to help you.'

'Thanks.' I reach out, and he takes my hand. 'For everything.'

He only nods and closes the door softly behind him. I stare after him for a long while, until the cooling T-shirt spurs me into action.

Everything takes a lot longer than it should, but with the support of the bathtub and the wall, I manage to shed my clothes in an untidy heap on the floor. I soon abandon my original plan of sitting on the edge as impractical and slide down the side to sit at the bottom of the tub. The warm water feels glorious against my hypersensitive skin, and I take my time as I wash my hair and rinse away any trace of last night's sickness. Showering clears my thoughts, which turn once again to the case at hand. For the first time, I catch the question that eluded me last night: who had the opportunity to poison Jessika and me?

Wolfsbane acts fast. Had someone sprinkled it on the breakfast buffet, the symptoms would have appeared hours before they did. Lunch is the only possible time, and sitting next to each other, we were easy targets. But who would have dared to attempt something like that in front a room full of people?

Perhaps it's simpler than that. The poison could have been smeared on the cutlery or around the rim of the glasses. There was no set seating plan for lunch, so it's possible the culprit didn't care about who the victims would be, only that someone would fall gravely ill.

Not many people would recognise the symptoms of wolfsbane poisoning, let alone know how to treat it. I was lucky to have Wishearth waiting for me in my room. Had he left or had I never called for his help in the first place, I could have died.

Sitting under the spray, I begin to shake. It reminds

me of the last time I sobbed in the shower after I had returned from my trip to the Unseen Lands. On that occasion I was lost, and frightened of the battle still ahead of me. This time, I am grateful to be alive.

How will I ever repay Wishearth for saving my life?

I have no answers, so I switch off the shower and wrap myself in the towel. It carries a faint scent of wood smoke, which soothes the tremors shuddering through me. I sit on the edge of the tub again as I dry myself and dress slowly in the clean clothes. My conscience twinges at leaving yesterday's clothes discarded on the floor, but I will put up the "do not disturb" sign on the door and tidy up later.

The shower has washed away some of the residual weakness from my limbs, and I manage to walk to the door unaided. When I open it, I find Wishearth pacing across the carpet. He whirls around, his shoulders relaxing when he spots me. A cloche-covered tray sits on the small table by the balcony, and he guides me to it.

'I ordered you breakfast from room service.'

'Great. I'm starving,' I say, and my stomach growls in confirmation.

When he lifts the cloche, my heart sinks. On the plate are two slices of toast and two boiled eggs. A glass of orange juice, a cup of coffee, and a bowl of fruit salad sit next to it.

'Did they run out of food downstairs?' I ask, unable to hide my disappointment.

'No, but you need to take things slow. The only reason I ordered coffee is because it will help clear any remains of the belladonna from your system.'

'Thanks, I guess.'

I'd like to complain, but in truth I am too hungry to object. It takes me no time to finish breakfast. I wonder whether it is too late to order some more, when Wishearth sets my phone down next to the tray.

'Karrion will be waiting to hear from you.'

In the haze of last night and this morning, I had forgotten about Karrion's call. When I switch on my phone, I find six increasingly-annoyed text messages from him. The last one accuses me of having fun without him. I dial his number and put the phone on speaker. Karrion answers straight away.

'Yan, finally. Where the hell have you been? Have you been rescuing damsels in distress without me?'

'I was poisoned.'

'That's no excuse not to return my... Wait. What?'

'I was poisoned. Yesterday lunchtime. Wishearth saved my life.'

On the opposite side of the table, Wishearth relaxes back in his seat, a satisfied smile spreading across his face. Perhaps he views Karrion more as a rival than I had realised. In this instance, Wishearth has the upper hand and he is enjoying every moment of it.

'If you don't tell me what's going on right now, I'm going to jump on the first train to Sussex and sit on you until you do.'

Karrion's threat is real enough that I relent and bring him up to speed on everything that has happened since we last spoke. To my surprise, he manages to keep quiet until I reach the end of my story, but not a second longer.

'Who would want to poison you? Do you have any leads? Is Jessika okay? Was Robbert poisoned too? Could it have been an accident? Was anyone else sick? Do you know who took the rings? Do you have a theory, you always have a theory, right?'

'Slow down, Karrion,' I say with a laugh. 'You're not trying to win speed records for the most questions in a single breath.'

'If I was, I'd win. But you're stalling. Tell me what you're thinking.'

Wishearth leans forward in his seat, resting his elbows on the table and leaning his chin into his fingers. He too wants to know my thoughts on the case.

'First up, I'm pretty sure we're dealing with two separate incidents.'

'What do you mean?' Karrion interrupts. 'Haven't there been four of them?'

'Yes, sorry, I wasn't being specific enough. I think there are two *sets* of incidents.'

'Do you mean two different people are involved?'

'There has been more than one person mixed up in this since the very beginning, but I do think there are two people responsible for trying to sabotage the wedding and they're not acting together.'

'What makes you say that?' Wishearth asks just as Karrion begins to speak.

'Wishearth?' Karrion asks. 'Are you there as well? I hadn't realised.'

'Sorry, I should have mentioned you're on speaker phone,' I say.

'No, it's fine. I was surprised, that's all.'

'Since her life is in danger, I decided that Yannia could do with someone watching her back.'

'If you need help, I'm happy to catch a train. What I said earlier to persuade you to talk may have been a joke, but I can come and help for real.'

'It's okay, I think you can be of more help in Old London. Have you discovered anything further about Dharren or about Robbert's family? Any reason why someone would want to stop the wedding?'

'I have some awesome gossip to tell you,' Karrion says, and I hear the grin in his voice.

'Go on then, amaze us.'

Although I am focused on the phone, I notice from the corner of my eye that Wishearth smiles at my choice of words.

'I looked into Dharren first, given that running his family's magical ingredient business makes him the obvious suspect. In this instance, though, I think the ink may have been a red herring.'

'Why?'

'With a little bit of polite Internet stalking, I discovered that he's currently spending time with his new girlfriend in Ibiza. Unless he hired someone else to do his dirty work, it couldn't have been him. Also, his girlfriend looks like she should be at school, not on a beach sipping cocktails with a much older man. I wonder if her parents know why Dharren's marriage ended in such a hushed-up divorce.'

'If they did, I doubt they would have let her go away with him,' I say.

'Let's hope not, though he is rich, so he may have his appeal if you like black eyes to go with your Cartier necklaces.'

'Anything else?'

'Not on Dharren,' Karrion says. 'Maybe I should have kept digging, but I figured he was likely to be the convenient scapegoat because of the family business and even

117

if he's a horrible person, he is probably innocent of this particular charge.'

'I agree.'

'So I spent last night searching around the Web for anything on Robbert's family. Aside from all the media attention surrounding the accident that killed his wife and children, there has been nothing terribly interesting about him in the news. But I found a strange opinion piece written by his sister Carrolyn, which sent me digging into her and her part in the family scene.'

'What was the opinion piece?' I ask. My stomach growls, and I wonder if Wishearth would be offended if I ordered more breakfast.

'It talked about how it was high time the old patriarchal norms of the society changed. That women may be equal on paper, but scratch the surface and the old Mage families still use money and tradition to keep women trapped in the prisons of home and motherhood. It was a bit harsh at times, but also made some good points. For some reason, it made me think of Lord Ellensthorne.'

'Now that you mention it, we've never seen a glimpse of Lady Ellensthorne. From the information Mr Whyte gave us on the Council, he's definitely married and has children too.'

'Knowing him, they're probably locked in the basement,' Karrion mutters.

'Be that as it may, I'm not sure what an opinion piece about the hidden gender inequalities of Old London has to do with the case,' I say.

'Nothing per se, but the tone of the article was sharp enough that it made me curious about the writer. That's when I looked up Carrolyn.'

'And?' I prompt him, trying not to sound too impatient.

'She's the most boring person on the planet based on her social media accounts. Pictures of flower arrangements and artisan cheeses. Who likes that stuff?'

'Probably someone with time and money to spare. Get to the point, Karrion.'

'Right, so I nearly gave up because there are only so many pictures of fresh Parmesan I can look at without thinking that my room smells like vomit, but there was an article that caught my eye. It's from years ago, but I guess the magic of the Internet search engines brought it back to people's attention after Carrolyn wrote her article. When Robbert and Carrolyn's father died, he left most of his estate to Robbert as his only son and heir. Carrolyn's share was put in a trust. She receives income from it, but the trustees control the assets. When she dies, the trust funds would have passed to her children, but since she doesn't have any, they revert back to Robbert and his descendants.'

'Mortals do like convoluting their affairs,' Wishearth says.

Ignoring Wishearth, I tap my fingers along the edge of the table while I consider the information. It is interesting, without a doubt, but does it have anything to do with this weekend's events? I'm not certain. How would the inheritance of assets she has no control over make her want to stop the wedding? None of it fits, yet I cannot help feeling Karrion is on the right track.

'Good work,' I say.

'Does it help?' he asks, a little breathless.

'I think so. It's another piece of the puzzle, but we're still missing something.'

'What's that?'

'No idea. That's the problem.'

'Whatever it is, I'm sure you'll figure it out, Yan.'

'I hope so. What about this hotel? Anything interesting there?'

'Not really. There were a few negative reviews posted online, but they were nonsense, like no sourdough toast available in the breakfast buffet, or that the koi in the pond weren't colourful enough. Stuff that no one in their right mind would complain about.'

'That's one dead end, then,' I say. 'Good. Disgruntled customers would have only complicated my thinking.'

'I'm serious about my offer, Yan. If you need help, just say the word and I'll be right over. I mean, in a few hours, but I'll definitely be there.'

'Thanks, Karrion. You're a big help. We'll keep you posted.'

I end the call and lean back in my chair. Wishearth is watching me with open curiosity.

'Why didn't you ask him to come?' he asks.

'Didn't you say I needed no other backup than you?' I ask, and my eyes stray to the empty plate in front of me.

'Yes, but I didn't think you'd take me seriously.'

'It's hard to tell with you sometimes.'

I rise and head for the bathroom. Hot fingers close around my wrist. I turn back as Wishearth stands, and we end up face to face.

'If it is serious you need, here goes: I will keep you safe as far as is within my power. But you must remember that I'm not mortal and as such, I have a great many limitations when operating in your world.'

His turn of phrase distracts me into wondering what

his home plane is like. No spirit is born on the mortal plane, and he is probably from the elemental world of fire. He has never said for certain and I have never thought to ask. Now is not the time, and I smile. In a brash moment of bravery, I lean forward and kiss his cheek.

'Thank you, Wishearth. I appreciate having you here to lend me your support.'

He squeezes my wrist briefly and lets go. I continue to the bathroom, turning his words over in my head. Wishearth is not one to admit weakness lightly, but he has been sharing more of himself with me over the past couple of months. To what end, I cannot tell.

# CHAPTER 12

'We should check how Jessika is,' I say, once I have brushed my teeth. The breakfast tray is no longer on the table.

Wishearth nods and follows me. We walk down the corridor. I am just about to knock on the bridal suite door when the lift pings and footsteps hurry towards us. A man carrying a heavy bag is approaching at a run, with Robbert behind him. Robbert's face is twisted with effort and fear.

'What's going on?' I ask, fearing that Wishearth delivered the cure too late.

'It's Calleigh. She collapsed.'

Robbert opens the door, and we follow him in. Jessika is sitting on the floor, wearing a fluffy bathrobe, Calleigh's head on her lap. The dog whimpers softly when she sees Robbert and offers a feeble wag of her tail.

The man, who I now understand to be a vet, kneels on the floor and unzips his bag. He examines Calleigh with gentle hands, murmuring softly the whole time. When he is finished, he looks up.

'How long has she been like this?'

'An hour,' Robbert says. 'I took her outside and she seemed a little reluctant, but happy to be with me. When we returned, her legs gave out.'

'Robbert?' A rising voice calls out from the doorway. 'What's going on?'

I turn to find Carrolyn standing there, immaculately dressed in a pale pink trouser suit. One of her hands is raised to her mouth as her eyes dart from Robbert's distress to the dog on the floor.

'Calleigh is not well.'

'I'm sorry to hear that, but shouldn't you be resting?'

'What?' Robbert frowns, shaking his head. 'Why?'

'You're not well either. I know how much you care about the dog, but in the grand scheme of things, your wellbeing is far more important than hers.'

Robbert clenches his teeth. 'It's been fifteen years since my accident. I'm fine.'

'There's no need to keep pretending.' Carrolyn crosses her arms and glares at Jessika. 'I know you're dying and that she's only marrying you for the family fortune.'

'What?' Robbert and Jessika ask in unison.

The sound of the argument fades away as the pieces of the puzzle click into place. This is what I was missing. I sway, caught up in the picture before my eyes, and a hot hand takes hold of my elbow. Casting a grateful glance in Wishearth's direction, I find him smiling at me.

'I'm glad I had the opportunity to see this,' he whispered, making sure no one else overhears us.

'See what?'

'You solving a case.'

I want to ask what he means, but he shakes his head. Wishearth is right. There will be time later to discuss this. For now, I must help Robbert and Jessika see the truth.

'Can you find Antonnio?' I ask Wishearth, careful to keep my voice low.

'The Cat Shaman?'

'Yes. Bring him here.'

Wishearth leaves without another word, but no one else in the room notices. The vet is injecting something into Calleigh's neck, while Jessika has risen to stand next to Robbert's wheelchair.

'This is madness,' Robbert says, 'I may be paralysed, but there's nothing wrong with me.'

'I overheard you,' Carrolyn shrieks. 'A month ago, when I was visiting for lunch. I was coming to say goodbye as you finished the telephone conversation. You said they had confirmed the cancer was terminal and there was nothing anyone could do. You were crying, and your gold-digger here said that together you'd see it through to the end. She would, wouldn't she? When she stands to inherit everything, even my trust fund after I'm gone.'

'It's Calleigh who has cancer, you stupid woman! And how dare you call my wife a gold-digger?'

'Not your wife yet and never going to be, if I have any say in the matter.'

'You don't,' Jessika says, her voice trembling, but her jaw is set.

Carrolyn is about to reply, when I step between them. 'Why don't we all back off and calm down. All this shouting is upsetting Calleigh. Once she's settled, we need to discuss the events of this weekend.'

'Trust an uncivilised monster like her to put a dog ahead of people,' Carrolyn sneers, but Robbert cuts her off.'

'Yannia is right. You,' he points to his sister, 'go sit over there and shut the fuck up.'

Although Carrolyn's expression is outraged, she does as she is told and seats herself on one of the armchairs. As angry as she may be, she still takes care to tuck one ankle behind the other and fold her hands on her lap. Robbert sees none of this, for he is leaning forward in his chair to stroke Calleigh's head.

'How bad is it?' he asks the vet.

'I'm afraid it's not good news. Based on the cancer diagnosis you told me about and her current medication, my feeling is that she has come to the end of her road. I've given her a shot of pain relief. She has, at most, days. My suggestion is that I give you extra pain relief so you can take her home, but after that, I would not let her suffer any longer.'

Robbert reaches for Jessika's hand. She is by his side in an instant, wrapping an arm over his shoulder.

'We're getting married today. But tomorrow, we'll let her go.'

'It's the right decision. I'll make sure you have everything you need to make her comfortable until then.'

'Thank you.'

The vet takes a medicine bottle for his bag and explains the dosage to Robbert, whose eyes remain fixed on Calleigh. The men shake hands, and the vet leaves. He passes Wishearth and Antonnio in the doorway.

'What are you doing here?' Carrolyn asks, staring at Antonnio.

'This man, he told me Robbert needed me.'

Wishearth shrugs, unconcerned by the confusion of the mortals now he has accomplished his task, but he does close the door and lean against it. The message is clear.

Robbert stays by Calleigh's side until her breathing evens and her eyes slip closed. We all move away to let her sleep.

'How are you feeling?' I ask Jessika.

'Better than yesterday.' She smiles at Wishearth. 'Your friend saved me.'

'He's been doing that a lot recently,' I say, and the flames in Wishearth's eyes flare high, illuminating his cheekbones.

'I just don't understand who'd do something as terrible as poisoning us.'

'I can shed light on that. Why don't you sit down and we can talk? We don't have long before you need to start getting ready.'

Jessika sits on the sofa, and Robbert wheels his chair to be next to her. I choose the other end of the sofa, while Antonnio folds himself into the remaining armchair.

'I think it best to keep this between us for now,' I say, feeling like a television detective about to reveal who the killer is. 'Once everything is out in the open, Robbert and Jessika can decide what they'd like to do.'

'The more I listen to you, the less I want to be here,' Carrolyn says, preparing to stand. 'Your Miss Marple charade has gone on long enough.'

'Sit.'

Robbert's tone brooks no refusals, and she settles back into the chair.

'You were so careful with your wording yesterday.' I turn to Antonnio, who arches a perfect eyebrow. 'A little too careful, actually, because what you said bothered me.'

'What did I say?' he asks without a hint of discomfort.

'That you never saw anyone enter or exit Jaike's room through the balcony.'

Antonnio shrugs. 'It is the truth.'

'Yes, it is.'

At last his composure cracks and he frowns. 'Then why are you so bothered about my words?'

'Because they were so precise. If you'd said that no one entered or exited through the balcony, I might not have thought twice about it. But you used the word "saw".'

'So?'

'You didn't see anyone go into Jaike's room because you were the one who stole the rings.'

Jessika jumps up. 'Why would you do that? You're one of Robbert's oldest friends.'

'I suspect he's after a story far bigger than the one he claims to be writing. Reporting on an aristocratic wedding is one thing, being the first one to break the news of a scandal within one of the most affluent families of Old London quite another. Something about a dying man and a woman seeking to steal the family's fortunes, am I right?'

Antonnio merely tilts his head, the ghost of a smile playing on his lips.

'That is how she,' I nod to Carrolyn, 'convinced you to play a part in all this, isn't it?'

'How dare you?'

This time, Robbert only glances her way and she says nothing further, though she crosses her arms and glares at me.

'Perhaps you've been bored in your profession as a reporter and wanted something a little more thrilling. Or perhaps this is how you've conducted your investigative journalism all along. You wouldn't be the first Cat Shaman to put your feline instincts to good use.'

'How did you know?' he asks, and I detect grudging respect in his voice.

'Besides the obvious hint you dropped when we spoke to you yesterday morning? You searching for your phone during lunch was a distraction. The only person it could have been for was Carrolyn, who arrived just in time to slip wolfsbane into mine and Jessika's soup.'

'You poisoned us?' Jessika sways. Robbert draws her back down to sit, staring in disbelief at his sister.

'How dare you try to kill my bride?'

'It was only a few drops of wolfsbane,' Carrolyn says, batting away Robbert's anger as if it was a fly. 'She was in no real danger. All I wanted was for her to be ill enough to miss the wedding.'

The smell of fresh branches on fire fills the room. Wishearth's outline shimmers with heat as he stalks across the room. His features are twisted beyond recognition, eyes blazing incandescent with rage. Carrolyn pales, shrinking against the back of the armchair.

'Yannia almost died,' he growls in a voice as slow as shifting lava. It sets my teeth on edge, and I am glad his anger is not directed at me. 'Had I not recognised the poison and obtained the antidote, she *would have* died.'

'She's little better than an animal—' Carrolyn says, but Wishearth leans towards her. The fabric of the armchair begins to smoke near his hands. 'I'm sorry. I'm sorry. Please don't burn me.'

He remains there for a few seconds before taking a step back. The scowl never leaves his face and his eyes continue to glow white.

'I can't believe you hate Jessika enough to poison her rather than see us marry,' Robbert says, shaking his head. 'I also can't believe I didn't notice how intolerant you've become over the years.'

'What do you expect, when I grew up in a household that told me every day how we are better than everyone else, only to turn around and show that I wasn't good enough to inherit anything from our parents outright? Even then our family was all I had. Now some divorcee is going to take it all away from me. This is not just the end of you, it will be the end of our line. How can you let that happen?'

'You make it sound like it's my fault Sussannah and the girls died. I never thought I'd find happiness again until I met Jessika.'

'Perhaps if you'd looked after your family a little better, they'd still be alive.'

Robbert raises a hand, pauses, and lets it drop onto his lap. 'I never thought Father's will could turn you so bitter. He left you ample provision and had you gone on to have a family of your own, they would have been well looked after.'

'It's not the same,' Carrolyn hisses. 'None of it was mine.'

'You should have been grateful for what you had instead of expecting more.' Robbert turns to me. 'Would you mind calling the Paladins? No doubt they'll have something to say about two counts of attempted murder.'

'You can't be serious.' Carrolyn leaps up, careful to keep the armchair between herself and Wishearth. 'You'd call the Paladins on your own sister?'

'As far as I'm concerned, you lost the right to call

yourself that the moment you began interfering with my wedding.'

I reach for my phone, but Carrolyn moves faster than I anticipated and knocks it out of my hand. It lands at Antonnio's feet. I have no time to try to recover it, for Carrolyn draws a curved dagger from her pocket, flicking the sheath to the floor, and points the tip of it at my side.

'Either you let me leave here unharmed, or she bleeds out on the carpet.'

# CHAPTER 13

Wishearth starts forward, but a warning look from me stops him. He clenches his hands into fists and the haze around him grows. His rage steadies me as I fight to remain completely still.

'Carrolyn, be reasonable,' Robbert says.

'I'm done being reasonable. Stay where you are, or I'll butcher this animal like she deserves.'

Robbert continues speaking, but I tune him out. The poison has left me weak, and my muscles tremble from the effort of not moving. But I have my inner reserves of power and I have no intention of letting Carrolyn out of this room except in chains.

I allow my aura to unfurl, seeking threads of power. Beyond the people around me, the first being I encounter is Calleigh. She is weak and I am about to move on, when I return to her. I take little from her, and her will to live steadies my muscles. There is hardly anything in the hotel that can bolster my magic and the gardens within my reach have little to do with wildness, but every blade of grass, every shrub has a thread of power. It is just enough.

My fingers contract into the claws of a lynx at the same time as I use the scales of an adder to protect my skin. The reflexes of a pine marten give me the speed I need. I spin to the side, bring my hands up, and sink the claws into

Carrolyn's forearm. She screams, leaving my ears ringing. Hot blood slides down my fingers as my claws rake her flesh. A dull thud signals the dagger landing on the carpet.

Carrolyn turns away from me, but we are linked by my grip. I snarl at her. If she is so determined to call me an animal, I will show her how feral I can be. After a Fey Lord, a South Mage is hardly a threat.

Before I have a chance to do more than bare my teeth, a fist connects with the side of Carrolyn's head, which snaps back. She falls to the ground, forcing me to let go. Antonnio stands beside her, his fist still raised.

'I changed my mind about wanting her story,' he says with a shrug, and returns to his chair. 'This, I believe, will be even more interesting.'

Wishearth rushes forward while my claws shimmer and retract. My hands are slick with Carrolyn's blood, and it's shockingly bright.

'It doesn't look like she cut you,' he says, examining my hands, and I allow the last of my magic to fade.

'No,' I reply, dazed by the events.

'I suggest you wash your hands before calling the Paladins. No point smearing blood all over your phone.'

'Right.'

His practicality shakes me out of my stupor, and I hurry to the bathroom. As I watch the water in the basin turn from deep red to pale pink, I marvel at another close call. Did Carrolyn have it in her to kill me? Slipping poison into my food was one thing, but perhaps actually stabbing me may have been a step too far for her. I try to find a measure of comfort in the thought.

When I return to the main room, Carrolyn is sitting up, a hand cradling the side of her face where Antonnio hit her. She regards us with open hostility, while Jessika glares back at her with equal venom. Wishearth has returned to guarding the door.

Robbert has wheeled himself forward, and he is staring at the dagger on the rug. 'It's from our father's collection.'

Jessika kneels next to him and hugs Robbert. He turns his head, hiding his expression from us.

To give them a measure of privacy, I retrieve my phone from the floor, where it landed, and call the Paladins. They promise to dispatch a section to Sussex immediately, and I end the call. I also call the local police. It will take some time before the Paladins arrive, and I am certain Carrolyn will attempt to flee if given half a chance. Humans cannot contain her long, but hopefully long enough. While I have been on the phone, Robbert has ordered each of us a brandy from room service. Antonnio reaches for a tumbler, but Robbert's hand closing around his wrist stops him.

'Where are my rings?' Robbert asks through clenched teeth.

'In my room,' Antonnio says. 'I shall retrieve them.'

Robbert looks between me and Wishearth, but Antonnio raises his hands.

'I shall be back. Gentleman's word.'

'You can hardly be called a gentleman.'

'Now is a good time to begin anew.'

When Robbert doesn't reply, Antonnio leaves. I glance at Wishearth, who nods, and fades from view.

True to his word, Antonnio returns moments later, carrying two ring boxes. I have been adding logs to the fire, and Wishearth takes shape next to me on the hearth stones. Together we watch as Antonnio presents the rings to Robbert.

'My apologies, Robbert. Though you should know that I never intended to keep them. The arrangement was that as soon as the wedding was off, I would hand them back to you and claim I found them outside in the garden.'

'That's something, I suppose. And while you're confessing to things, were you the one who ruined Jessika's wedding dress and put the doves in the dining room?'

Confusion flickers over Antonnio's features, prompting me to return to the others. I pick up one of the brandy tumblers from the tray and sit on the sofa. Wishearth comes to stand behind me, a hand resting on my shoulder. I am grateful for his warmth.

'Antonnio had nothing to do with those incidents,' I say, sipping my brandy. 'Neither did Carrolyn.'

'How do you know?' asks Robbert.

My gaze flickers to Jessika on the other end of the sofa. 'I have a hunch.'

'Jessika?' Robbert turns to her. 'What does Yannia mean?'

'How did you know?' she asks me.

Reaching into the pocket of my jeans, I withdraw two grey feathers. 'These. You're allergic to down. It makes your eyes water and your nose run.'

'What's going on?' Robbert asks, and takes Jessika's hand.

I smile at them both. 'One of the first things Jessika told me about you on Friday was your love of fictional detectives. Arranging for you to play a private detective for the weekend was an unusual wedding present, but you can't fault Jessika's creativity.'

Robbert's eyes widened. 'You set up the pranks?'

'Yes,' she says. 'You were so excited about meeting Yannia and I knew that you shadowing her on one of her real cases would be impractical, so I decided to create a case for you to solve. I bribed one of the waiters to help me. Only, none of it went as planned.'

'You weren't to know that someone wanted to sabotage your wedding for real,' I say. 'Which is why you were genuinely upset when you heard about the stolen rings.'

Jessika turns to Robbert. 'I hope you're not angry with me? You seemed to glow while you and Yannia were investigating the pranks.'

'You went to all that trouble so I could play detective for the weekend?'

'Technically, you stopped playing yesterday morning, when the rings were stolen,' I say. 'At that point, you became a real detective.'

Robbert draws Jessika into a hug. Although I try not to eavesdrop, my sharp hearing catches the words he murmurs into her hair.

'You're extraordinary. I love you.'

'I love you too.' She kisses him.

'But what about your wedding dress?' Robbert asks. 'It can't be salvaged.'

'It doesn't matter. My mother picked out that dress for me, and I hated it. This way I can wear the dress I like without her causing a scene.'

Jessika rises and walks to the wardrobe. A white garment bag hangs on the inside of the door. She unzips it to reveal a simple ivory dress with narrow sleeves. It is elegant and understated, far more Jessika's style than the other one.

'I left it in Old London until this morning, when my housekeeper drove it down.'

'It's beautiful. I'm guessing the runes you painted onto the old dress were a blessing for a long marriage.' I drain the last of my brandy.

Jessika smiles at Robbert. 'And a happy one.'

With a glance at my phone to check the time, I rise. 'On that note, we'd better leave you to get ready.'

'Wait,' Robbert says. 'There's one thing we need to do before the ceremony, and we'd like you to be here for it.'

'Of course.'

After a nod from Robbert, Jessika rises and fetches a large object wrapped in brown paper from the bathroom. She stops by the fireplace, and we follow her there. Robbert helps her unwrap the paper to reveal a wreath of bay leaves, tied with ivy, with a red and white rose at the centre. I have spent enough time with Lady Bergamon to have learned something about the hidden meanings of plants. Robbert and Jessika hold a bay wreath to recognise merit, ivy for marriage, and red and white roses together for unified love. I share a smile with them.

Holding the wreath before him, Robbert leans closer to the fire. 'Hearth Spirit, a faithful guardian of all those who believe, we thank you for your protection and for saving my beloved bride. Bless this marriage so that we may grow old together.'

The wreath burns bright, and the flames are reflected in Wishearth's eyes as he comes to stand behind Robbert and Jessika. They turn to him, and he lays a hand on each of their shoulders.

'May your marriage be blessed by the spirits who watch over this plane. No future is certain, but if you bind your lives together, you will have love, laughter, and joy for many years to come.'

Robbert and Jessika have tears in their eyes as they look at each other. I hope they will receive everything Wishearth predicts and more. They both deserve a second chance at happiness.

'Thank you,' Robbert says, his voice scratchy.

'We'll leave you to it.' I say, taking a step towards the door. 'See you at the ceremony.'

I walk to the door, Wishearth beside me, and I press it closed behind me. We share a smile as we return to my room.

'Will you come to the wedding?' I ask while swiping my key card.

'An aristocratic Mage wedding with lots of snooty barons and earls? I wouldn't miss it for the world.'

'Should I be worried?'

'Always.'

I laugh as I open the wardrobe and take out my dress. 'Do you still think I should have called Karrion for back-up?'

'No. We make a pretty good team.'

'Agreed.' I send Wishearth a crooked smile over my shoulder. 'Though remind me never to piss you off. You can be pretty terrifying when you're angry.'

'More so than a murder of crows?' he asks with a chuckle.

'Even a plague of pigeons.'

'I'll tell Karrion you said so.'

'Feel free. That way he can be annoyed at us both.'

I retreat to the bathroom before Wishearth has a chance to reply.

When I emerge much later, he is lounging on his usual spot on the sofa. Instead of the jeans, black jumper and mariner's pea coat he was wearing when I went into the bathroom, he is now dressed in a black suit with a flame red tie. Upon seeing me, he rises and grins.

'You clean up pretty well,' he says.

'Thanks. You sure know how to compliment a girl.'

'I've had centuries of practice.'

'Shouldn't that mean you ought to be better at it by now?'

'Is that any way to greet your faithful Hearth Spirit?'

'No.' On an impulse, I press a quick kiss on his cheek and drape a pale blue pashmina around my shoulders. 'You look good. Shall we?'

'Let's.'

Downstairs, the doors to the ballroom stand open and two ushers are handing out orders of services to the guests. Rows of chairs are arranged on both sides of an aisle of red carpet. There are white roses everywhere. Robbert is at the front of the room, adjusting his tie. He spots us when we enter, and we wave at him before choosing seats in the back row.

As we sit, Wishearth pulls up the scarf that has slipped off my shoulder, letting his fingers stroke my bare skin. His eyes are serious as he regards me.

'You look beautiful, Yannia.'

'Thank you.'

The room seems to grow several degrees hotter as we regard each other. I am only vaguely aware of the string quartet near us beginning to play. Wishearth's fingers entwine with mine as we stand to watch Jessika walk down the aisle.

# ACKNOWLEDGEMENTS

I am, as ever, indebted to Louise Walters not just for her faith in my series, but also for her support, guidance, and friendship. The series wouldn't be where it is without you. Thank you also to Leigh Forbes and Jennie Rawlings for turning a stack of pages into a book with a beautiful cover.

My heartfelt thanks to Andrew Rogers, who is as invested in my characters' journeys as I am and who is always up for reading another story. He remains my rock. Many thanks also to my family, who are racing through my published books and are telling me to hurry up and write faster. To have their support from afar means the world to me.

Thank you to all my readers for continuing to ask what happens next. As long as you keep asking, I'll have to keep coming up with answers.

Finally, thank you to Halla and Usva, my two shadows, who have big paw prints to fill.

# AUTHOR'S NOTE

A couple of years ago, I listened to all the Sherlock Holmes stories one after the other. Having been an avid Agatha Christie fan for years, her books and the Sherlock Holmes collection left me wanting to write a Wilde Investigations story set outside of Old London in a fancy country hotel. It was originally meant to be a short story for my newsletter, but I had barely set the scene and the word count was already past 6k, which is proof that short fiction is not my forte.

Although I had the main points of the story outlined in my mind, life happened and I set it aside for nearly a year and half. Last year, dodging lockdowns, I had a meeting with Louise where we discussed the future plans for my series and she suggested that we bring out a novella in 2021 to make up for the gap in between *Roots of Corruption* and *Wildest Hunger*. I outlined the plot for the novella and with Louise's encouragement, resurrected it. *The Doves in the Dining Room*, though it had a working title that sucked at the time, became one of my NaNoWriMo projects, which was all the motivation I needed to finish it. While I worked on the story, I swore blindly it would be 20k max, while my first reader calmly shook his head and told me I wouldn't get it done under 30k. He was, as always, right.

*The Doves* is a slight departure from the other books in the Wilde Investigations series in that while the characters possess magic, the solution to the mystery is altogether mundane. In that sense, it is a nod towards the great crime stories I so admire. It was also meant to be a one-off foray into the world of novellas, but Louise and my first reader have dropped enough hints that I may have to branch out a little. It doesn't take much to nudge me onto a tangent, especially when I have two wonderful people enabling me.

# Fallible Justice

### Laura Laakso

*"I am running through the wilderness
and the wilderness runs through me."*

IN OLD LONDON, where paranormal races co-exist with
ordinary humans, criminal ver-
dicts delivered by the all-see-
ing Heralds of Justice are
infallible. After a man is declared guilty of murder and
sentenced to death, his daughter turns to private investigator
Yannia Wilde to do the impossible and prove the Heralds
wrong.

Yannia has escaped a restrictive life in the Wild Folk
conclave where she was raised, but her origins mark her
as an outsider in the city. Those origins lend her the sen-
sory abilities of all of nature. Yet Yannia is lonely and
struggling to adapt to life in the city. The case could be
the break she needs. She enlists the help of her only
friend, a Bird Shaman named Karrion, and together they
accept the challenge of proving a guilty man innocent.

So begins a breathless race against time and against
all conceivable odds. Can Yannia and Karrion save a man
who has been judged infallibly guilty?

This is fantasy at its literary, thrilling best, and is the first title in Laura Laakso's paranormal crime series Wilde Investigations. There is a wonderfully human element to Laura's writing, and her work is fantasy for readers who don't like fantasy (or think they don't!) and it's perfect, of course, for those who do.

Available in paperback, e-book, and audio.

# *Echo Murder*

## Laura Laakso

*"I'm part of every bird I meet,*
*and they are all within me."*

YANNIA WILDE RETURNS to the
Wild Folk conclave where she
grew up, and to the deathbed
of her father, the conclave's
Elderman. She is soon drawn
back into the Wild Folk way of
life and into a turbulent relationship with Dearon, to
whom she is betrothed.

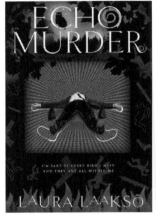

Back in London, unassum-
ing office worker Tim Wedgebury is surprised when police
appear on his doorstep with a story about how he was
stabbed in the West End. His body disappeared before the
paramedics' eyes. Given that Tim is alive and well, the police chalk the first death up to a Mage prank. But when Tim
"dies" a second time, Detective Inspector Jamie Manning
calls Yannia and, torn between returning to the life she
has built in Old London and remaining loyal to the conclave and to Dearon, she strikes a compromise with the
Elderman that allows her to return temporarily to the city.

There she sets about solving the mystery of Tim's
many deaths with the help of her apprentice, Karrion.

They come to realise that with every death, more of the echo becomes reality, and Yannia and Karrion find themselves in increasing danger as they try to save Tim. Who is the echo murderer? What sinister game are they playing? And what do they truly want?

The second in Laura's Wilde Investigations picks up where *Fallible Justice* left off, transporting us once again to Laura's vividly re-imagined London... and for the first time to the Wild Folk conclave which has such an emotional pull on Yannia... a fabulous second-in-the-series novel.

Available in paperback, e-book, and audio.

# *Roots of Corruption*

## Laura Laakso

*"What could Lady Bergamon have to fear
in a garden of her own making?"*

ON THE NIGHT of Samhain, the veil between worlds is at its thinnest, and ancient magic runs wild in Old London.

When Lady Bergamon is attacked in her Ivy Street garden, Wishearth turns to Yannia for help. Who could have the power to harm Lady Bergamon in her own domain? While Yannia searches for the answer, nature herself appears to be killing Mages in Old London. Yannia and Karrion join forces with New Scotland Yard to solve the baffling Mage deaths. But wherever they turn, all the clues point back towards Ivy Street.

Yannia's abilities are put to the test as she races to save Lady Bergamon's life, and prevent further murders. But with the lines between friends and enemies blurring, she must decide who to trust and how much she's willing to sacrifice for Old London and its inhabitants.

Available in paperback, e-book, and audio.
**Longlisted in the inaugural Barbellion Prize 2020**

Coming in autumn 2022...

# *Wildest Hunger...*
## the fourth Wilde Investigations novel

THE OLDEST AND GRAVEST of the Wild Folk laws dictates that human flesh must not be consumed. When half-eaten bodies start turning up between Old London and the North, Yannia Wilde knows the killer can only be one of her kind. Yannia's investigation is even more complicated when her betrothed, Dearon, insists on joining forces with her and Karrion.

While Yannia tries to balance tracking down the killer with the tension between her and Dearon, and Karrion, another case in Old London draws her attention. A West Mage Council member, whom Yannia exposed as a Leech only days before, has gone missing, and his girlfriend is found murdered in his flat. Is the Leech, a master of deception, capable of murder, or has someone framed him?

Caught in the web of Old London's political intrigue, Yannia must learn to play the game and to choose her allegiances with care. But to catch a predator of her kind, she must also embrace her wildness and set aside everything that makes her human.

And we are thrilled to share with you here the opening chapter of *Wildest Hunger...*

# 1

## RIPPLES

The map of Old London rustles in the breeze, its edge catching on the brim of my tourist hat. Through the gap between them, I watch as a group of Mages strides across the square. Their destination is the marble-clad Guildhall behind me, the administrative centre of Old London and the place where the High Council of Mages has been meeting for centuries. The Mages' cloaks marking them as Council members flutter in their wake. A light breeze blows their scent towards me.

Hidden behind my disguise, I allow the forked tongue of a snake to sample the air: two West Mages and a South Mage.

No Leeches.

My task of vetting the High Council of Mages is almost complete, and so far I have found no one masquerading as a Mage. With every name I tick off my list, I am wondering more and more whether Gideor Braeman was the solitary exception. But Lord Wellaim Ellensthorne as the Speaker is paying a premium fee for my services and I have every reason to be thorough.

A glance at my watch shows that the Council meeting has begun. Anyone in attendance will have arrived already. Time for me to leave.

I am straightening the map to fold it, when running footsteps draw my attention back to the square. A young man in the earthy green cloak of an East Mage is hurrying towards the Guildhall. Right before he passes by, his scent reaches me, sour and strange. Even without resorting to the power in my blood, my brain gives him a name: a Leech.

The map rustles while my body shudders and adrenaline floods my veins. I want to call upon the claws of a lynx and the teeth of a bear to defend myself, although they would be of no use against a Leech. It has been nearly two months since Jans broke into my flat, and yet the sour tang of a Leech is enough to send my pulse tripping and for bile to rise in my throat. I search my memory for a name: Gerreint Lloid. He is one of the newer members of the Council and one I thought was high risk. I was right.

Aside from the initial tremor in my hands, I force my expression to remain neutral as I turn away and fold the map. It will not do for a PI to show their emotions. In Old London, someone is always watching. As I leave the square, I hesitate by a bin, but opt to keep my disguise. I have not yet finished vetting the Circle of Shamans. The tourist outfit may come in handy.

When my calves begin to ache and my knee jars, I realise I have been rushing to reach my car. A glance over my shoulder shows nothing out of the ordinary. Why should there be, when the Leech did not notice me in his haste to get to the meeting? Yet my breathing only evens when I close the car door and lock it behind me.

Scrolling through the contacts on my phone I select one. When the call connects, I skip all niceties.

'Mr Whyte, I found a Leech.'

Once home, I hurry through my damp office and up the stairs. Lady Bergamon is due to visit, and I want to make sure the house is tidy. When I open the door to the lounge, Sinta trots to greet me. She comes halfway across the room before squatting. I pick up a clean rag from a pile by the fireplace and lay it on the puddle. Scooping her up, I open the lounge window and climb out. She reaches to lick my chin.

How strange to come home to find I have been missed so.

I set Sinta down, and she spends a long while sniffing at the individual blades of grass before the few remaining leaves clinging to a blackcurrant bush arrest her attention. She bounds across the small lawn and leaps at the leaves. In the past month, she has grown. Her wobbly bat ears still look disproportionate, but her body has lengthened. She is beginning to look more like the corgi she is rather than a ball of fluff with giant ears. Her attention span remains that of a puppy, and she soon loses interest in the leaves. She also seems to have no interest in going to the toilet now she is outside.

Back in the lounge, I have enough time to clean up after Sinta and set the kettle to boil before the doorbell rings. Sinta howls, and I silence her with a finger on her nose. She tries to follow me down the stairs, and closing the door in front of her earns me another howl.

Lady Bergamon is dressed in a heavy wool cloak and her white hair is just visible under the fur-trimmed hood. I catch a few notes of 'Santa Baby' from a passing car. I step aside to invite her in, and she sets down her basket while she unclasps the cloak and hands it to me. She watches me with a smile as I hang the cloak on my coat stand. Her face is thinner than I recall, almost gaunt, and her aura has an uneven feel to it. When she draws me into a hug, her strength surprises me. She has not yet recovered from the attack on her garden, but at least she appears to be on the mend. I let my relief show in my smile.

'How are your hands?' she asks.

I flex them, and they twinge. The burn of Baneacre's rot is still fresh in my memory. It has been nearly three weeks since Lady Bergamon declared the healing had progressed far enough that I no longer needed to visit her every day. Between her herbs and magic, the cold iron tokens, and the antibiotics, the Fey infection has subsided. Like the knife wound on my side, the burns that covered my hands have faded to silvery scar tissue. The healing skin is tight, but a huge improvement on the weeping sores I had to begin with.

'A little tender, but much better.'

'That will ease over time,' Lady Bergamon says as she follows me upstairs. 'Fey magic is tricky. Any lingering effects from the wolfsbane?'

'None, thanks to you and Wishearth.'

'Good.'

As soon as we step into the lounge, Sinta rushes to Lady Bergamon. Her expression is one of adoration, which I thought was reserved for Funja and Wishearth. Although they have never met, Sinta is smitten.

'Wishearth told me you'd adopted a puppy.' Lady Bergamon strokes Sinta, who squirms and whimpers. 'He was quite taken with her.'

'From what I gathered, Wishearth conspired with

Funja to make sure Sinta came to me.'

'You could share your life with someone far worse.'

'Sinta is quickly showing that to be true.' I smile as I head towards the kitchen. 'Tea?'

'Please.' Lady Bergamon follows me. 'I have your father's medicine.'

'Thanks. When I go to the conclave, I'll bring back the last batch of bottles.'

'That would be helpful, otherwise I shall be required to drink more wine.'

We share a laugh while I prepare a pot of tea and place mugs and a plate of custard creams on the table. I study Lady Bergamon as she pours milk into her tea; the only sounds in the room the clink of our spoons and Sinta gnawing on a calf hoof. The lines around Lady Bergamon's eyes and mouth are deeper than when we first met, and in them, I read a tale of pain and regret. When she catches me staring, there is fatigue in her eyes.

'How are you?' I ask.

'Time is the greatest healer of all,' she says with forced brightness. When I offer no response, she busies herself with selecting a biscuit which she dunks in her tea. 'Truth be told, I haven't been sleeping well. The worst part of all is that I know I'll soon feel better.'

I wait for her to continue, but when she says nothing further, I shake my head. 'I don't understand.'

'The guilt I now feel, the sorrow, the anger at having been so helpless will fade until I will struggle to remember why I was so sad.'

'How much of your life do you remember?'

It was not what I intended to ask. I cover my uncertainty by lifting the mug to my lips while I wait to see whether my question has offended her.

'I remember a great deal, especially major events. But names and faces fade over time. My plants help with that.'

'You can store memories in your plants?'

Lady Bergamon laughs, and the sound is the rustle of silver birch leaves in a gentle breeze. 'Nothing like that. But scent has a great ability to unlock lost memories. I find natural smells far more potent than any others.'

As I dip my chin, my mind conjures recalled scents of heathered hills, fog-clad lakes, and fresh kills.

'And I imagine many of your memories are connected to the natural world.'

'Indeed.'

I want to ask her again what she is. Last time the subject came up, she admitted to not being a Plant Shaman, but said nothing further. I have an inkling of what the truth might be, but I am hesitant to present my theories to her.

Lady Bergamon pets Sinta, who responds by rolling over. She is rewarded with long fingers tickling her belly. One of her back paws beats a rhythm of pleasure against the table leg.

'It's good you have company. We could all do with an occasional break from solitude.' Lady Bergamon straightens in her seat.

'Are you lonely in your house and your garden?' I had not intended to blurt out the question either and as soon as I do, I fear I have overstepped the boundaries of our friendship.

A smile lifts the fatigue from her face as she regards me. 'I have my plants and Bradán for company. With visits from you and Wishearth, what else would I need?'

153

Her words prompt an image of Bradán roaming her garden, protecting both their domain and his lover from intruders. Only, he could not stop the decay Baneacre inflicted, nor could he reverse the spell on Lady Bergamon. Does a Fey feel guilt like we mortals do? How long before he forgets?

But, I soon realise that she did not answer my question. I do not push the matter further. If she wants to confide in me, I trust she will.

Lady Bergamon finishes her tea and sets down the mug. 'I shan't keep you any longer. You have a long drive ahead of you, and the work of a gardener is never finished.'

She helps me carry the crockery back to the kitchen, empties her basket, and tops up my jar of pain-relieving tea. As we head downstairs, I tell her what has been occupying a part of my mind during her visit.

'I found another Leech in the Council.'

Lady Bergamon twists to look at me, fingertips resting against the staircase wall. 'Did they spot you?'

'No. He was in a rush to get to the Council meeting.'

She turns to continue down, but not before I see the tight press of her lips. Once I have helped her don the cloak, she presses a kiss on my cheek.

'You must take care, my dear. A Leech is a dangerous creature at the best of times, and with influence among the Council and threatened with exposure, there's no telling what he'll do.'

'I'll be careful,' I say, smiling to try to dispel her unease. 'Besides, I'm fleeing the city for a few days.'

'No bad thing, I believe.' Lady Bergamon picks up her basket. 'Do call around when you're back and have a spare moment. And bring Sinta with you.'

154

I promise to do so, and we say our goodbyes. Leaning against the door frame, I watch her ascend the stairs to the street until the chill of the day forces me to shut the door.

The sound of my phone ringing causes me to rush upstairs, ignoring the ominous crunch from my left knee. Sinta is barking at the window, and I shush her as I pick up the phone. It is Detective Inspector Jamie Manning. I hesitate, conscious of how distant he has been of late. We have not spoken since the case involving Baneacre was wrapped up more than a month ago and I told him everything I held back during the investigation. I answer the call.

'Hi, Yannia,' he says, and my awkwardness is mirrored in his tone.

'Hello, Jamie. What can I do for you?'

'I was hoping to ask your opinion on some crime scene photos that have found their way to me. They're baffling, but you're the expert on all things natural.'

'Are they urgent?' I ask, and transfer my father's medicine into a canvas bag. Despite the paper wrapping, the bottles clunk against each other.

'Not terribly. If you could give me your thoughts sometime in the next couple of days, that would be great.'

'Sure. I'm heading up north for a brief visit to the conclave, but I should be back tomorrow evening.'

'Everything all right with your family?' Some of the formal edge in Jamie's voice gives way to curiosity.

'Fine. I just need to drop something off and make an appearance.'

I have never told Jamie who my father is or about the promises that bind me. Now is not the time to enlighten him.

'Right. I'll email those photos to you now. Call me

when you're ready to share your thoughts.'

Some of the awkwardness returns when Jamie says goodbye, and I am relieved to slip the phone in my back pocket. While my laptop boots, I pack my rucksack and check I have the medication I need. The email arrives as I am feeding Sinta. It contains nothing but Jamie's standard email signature and a zipped folder. I start the download while I pack the car. Although there is no urgency with the photos, I click on the first to discover what kind of crime scene Jamie needs my help with.

It is a death, possibly a murder. The field and the body barely register as my eyes are drawn to the tracks around the body. I stare at the photo until Sinta leaping on a squeaky toy pheasant pulls me from my preoccupation and I close the laptop lid. With the laptop under one arm and Sinta under the other, I leave. Sinta takes her place on the front seat with the certainty born out of two previous car journeys, and I fasten her harness to the belt. Even as I pet her and start the car, my mind's image of the photo never fades.

All the people listed here took out subscriptions and in doing so helped me enormously as a publisher. Subscriptions are not currently on offer, but please see my website for all the ways you can support Louise Walters Books.

**louisewaltersbooks.co.uk**

Heartfelt thanks to:

Claire Allen
Edie Anderson
Karen Ankers
Francesca Bailey-Karel
Tricia Beckett
JEJ Bray
Melanie Brennan
Tom & Sue Carmichael
Liz Carr
Penny Carter-Francis
Pippa Chappell
Eric Clarke
Karen Cocking
Louise Cook
Deborah Cooper
Tina deBellegarde
Giselle Delsol
James Downs
Jill Doyle
Kathryn Eastman
Melissa Everleigh
Rowena Fishwick

Harriet Freeman
Diane Gardner
Ian Hagues
Andrea Harman
Stephanie Heimer
Debra Hills
Henrike Hirsch
Claire Hitch
Amanda Huggins
Cath Humphris
Christine Ince
Julie Irwin
Merith Jones
Seamus Keaveny
Moon Kestrel
Ania Kierczyńska
Anne Lindsay
Michael Lynes
Karen Mace
Anne Maguire
Marie-Anne Mancio
Karen May

Cheryl Mayo
Jennifer McNicol
MoMoBookDiary
Rosemary Morgan
Jackie Morrison
Louise Mumford
Trevor Newton
Aveline Perez de Vera
Mary Picken
Helen Poore
Helen Poyer
Clare Rhoden
Rebecca Shaw
Gillian Stern

John Taylor
Julie Teckman
Sarah Thomas
Sue Thomas
Mark Thornton
Penny Tofiluk
Mary Turner
Ian Walters
Steve Walters
Charles Waterhouse
Elizabeth Waugh
Alexis Wolfe
Finola Woodhouse
Louise Wykes